I0567671

Saint Charles Place
An O Line Mystery

M. Saylor Billings

Billibatt Productions

Saint Charles Place - An O Line Mystery

Copyright© 2010 by M. Saylor Billings

Library of Congress Catalog Card Number: 2011912704

ISBN: 09838061-0-1
ISBN 13: 978-0-9838061-0-3
Billibatt Productions
www.billibatt.com
olinemysteries@gmail.com

DEDICATION

This book is dedicated to Raejean.

~With affection.

TABLE OF CONTENTS

ACKNOWLEDGMENT

The author gratefully acknowledges Nina Greeley for her generosity. It is through her tireless efforts and encouragement that *The O Line Mystery Series* has been brought to print. Thank you.

PROLOGUE

While the eight or so commuters waited for their public transit bus, they busied themselves with newspapers, mp3 players, coffee cups, or neck scarves. In turn, heads jerked up at the passing traffic. Just checking. Casually they shifted their weight before glancing down at their watches or cell phones for the time. The wet fog that encircled them began to dissipate. The dull grey sky awoke as yellow shafts of light passed between white billowing clouds that stretched and lulled along. A deep metallic hum announced the arrival of the O Line bus that would shuttle them from Ohlone Island into San Francisco via the Bay Bridge.

Michael Chan looked up from his newspaper in time to see the tall white rectangular bus sail triumphantly around the bend. He watched his fellow passengers jockey themselves into a haphazard boarding line. The bus halted with a jerk and the doors popped open. One by one each passenger placed a piece of plastic on top of the money taker, while the accompanying green light indicated acceptance. Or they would place dollar bills into the machine, which beeped as they shuffled deeper into the rectangle. Michael pulled out the three crisp dollar bills and fed the machine. He moved awkwardly around a passenger who stood in the aisle at the front of the bus, unwavering and unconcerned that they were obstructing the ingress.

At the next stop, a woman who sat below his strap hanging arm looked up at him. He maneuvered around to let her out and took her seat. He sat next to an older man with a five o'clock shadow, stringy long hair, and dressed in a flannel tie-dyed shirt and khakis.

"You look like a geriatric hippy." Michael said under his breath as he unfolded the newspaper.

"You look like an office coolie." The older man retorted moving his lips imperceptibly.

The two men sat unmoving and unspeaking for the next three stops until they reached the Warner tunnel that would take them under the Oakland Estuary. When the tunnel spit them out in the heart of Oakland's Chinatown, they had made the exchange. Michael folded his newspaper and got off at the next stop.

As he made his way through the crowded streets of Chinatown, he unfolded a small sheet of paper he had cupped in his hand. *Slip 23 Cove Point Basin.* He rolled up the paper between his fingers to toss it on the street but then stopped himself and slipped it into his pants pocket. He entered the Happy Lucky Café nodding at the staff and took a table against the wall.

As he pulled out a PDA, a waitress brought over hot tea and water. He took a thin memory card from his shirt pocket and inserted it into the side of the digital device. After his jok porridge was served, he settled down to read the downloaded classified documents and memos on his device.

The marina at Cove Point Basin is a desolate looking place. Aside from removal of the detritus that accumulates in former manufacturing areas, little care had been taken to make it attractive to the boat slip renters. There were no showers, no walking paths, and no security cameras. It was, in fact, a parking lot for boats. From the bus stop, Michael walked the half-mile or more to the marina where he came upon the walking bridge that led past a security gate to the boat slips. The security gate and number pad lock looked newer than the bridge. He looked closer at the number pad and remembered the sheet of paper he had wadded up in his pocket. He shook his head in frustration, pulled out the rolled-up wad from his pocket and carefully straightened it in the palm of his hand. Pressing his lips together he gathered spittle in his mouth and dripped it onto the paper. As he gently rubbed the spittle over the paper, a four-digit number appeared. He typed the number into the keypad and heard the door unlatch.

Slip 23 contained a shiny forty-foot fiberglass sloop. Michael wasn't sure whether to knock on the hull or call out for permission to board. The smell of diesel fuel and salty sea air mingled with the scent of the fragrant wild fennel that grew along the shoreline. He looked down at his black-soled loafers and at the white fiberglass hull. He glanced around casually at the other boats before slipping off his loafers. The lumber was cold beneath his feet and he picked up his loafers before climbing across the small span to the boat's deck. He knocked on the hatch and bent down to look through the small window on the side of the boat.

"Whadcha lookin' fer?" The gravelly voice came from the dock. Michael lost his footing but caught himself on the small rail that ran along the boat's edge. He looked up. Now, the older man from the bus was wearing a curly black wig with a black captain's hat perched on top.

"You look like a – " he paused. Signals and countersigns slipped from his consciousness. There were no words to accurately or insultingly describe what stood before him. Aside from the wig and hat, the older man was now wearing a wrap-around skirt, something perhaps from the Polynesian

Islands, and a rugby shirt over a fake pot belly that tilted unnaturally. With his mouth agape, Michael shook his head, "You just look mentally ill."

"You look like a wife beater," said the older man. "And you're on the wrong boat."

Michael stood up and looked over to the sign with the numbers 20-30 and counted down the row. "No I'm not."

"Evens are on that side. Odds are on this side. You're on slip number 26. You're so off base I had to come and get you."

Michael was infuriated but followed the man to the correct boat slip and boarded an older looking cruiser.

"You like boats?" He asked Michael.

"No."

He handed Michael what looked like two thin arm sweatbands and growled, "Put them on with the plastic on the inside. Like this." He showed Michael his own wrists.

They clamored down the hatch of the sloop.

The old man removed his disguise revealing a bald head and a medium build under the fake potbelly.

"So it's easier to dress older than younger." Michael said trying to impress the older field agent with his keen observation skills.

"For me. But for you? With that bone structure you could go as a woman." The vocal growl was gone and the old man spoke clearly for the first time.

Michael was disgusted. It was so easy for these old white guys to just start off by emasculating an Asian.

"I'm not emasculating you, son." The old man caught Michael's eye. "You don't think I'd dress up as a woman if I could get away with it? Grow up."

Michael said nothing but looked around the boat cabin as the old man closed the door to the hatch.

"You hungry?" He asked Michael.

"No, I had breakfast," Michael said but added, "but I could use a coffee or something."

"Good, me too. Fix us something." The old man busied himself with removing a small panel from the wall. "This area is turning into a lawless hotbed and it's going to get a lot worse. We've got a lot to go over."

"I'm glad to hear it. Nobody has told me anything, just that bunch of files and memos from the fraud division you gave me this morning." Michael said as he opened cabinets in the galley.

The old man unlatched a portal and aimed a remote at the boat next to his. Michael heard the muted music from the other boat turn on and looked up, the old man nodded at the other boat and grinned, "Always know your exits, son."

"So," Michael measured out the coffee grounds as he spoke, "what do you do here?"

"My job is to make sure information sold to the government stays inside the government." The old man sat down at the galley booth and spread out folders on the table in front of him as Michael finished filling the small coffee maker and turned it on. Michael grabbed a couple of bottles of water, placed them on the table, and scooted into the opposite side of the rounded booth.

"The reason nobody has told you anything is because there are only four people who know what's going on and we're two of those people. You're fairly new to this business - you don't have much field background, no ties to other agents, no financial difficulties, and you're a digital forensics expert - so you're the perfect candidate. Who did your field training?"

"Agent Cousineau."

"Ah, Big Cousin."

"You know him?"

"Sure. He's one of the best trainers we have. Hands down." The old man smiled. "He's still teaching Moscow Rules?"

Michael laughed. "Yeah."

"Look, I'm going to tell you straight off, there are a lot of ways to make some extra cash with this operation. Don't do it, ever. You *will* get burned." The old man opened his bottle of water. "You are going to be the whole of this operation. You're going to have to make your own contacts, informants, your own drops, everything."

Michael was not happy with this news. "Wait a minute, hang on, I'm being transferred out of IT? I didn't put in for a transfer."

"No, this a promotion. It's a career builder."

"To what, the *fraud* division?" Michael had worked very hard to place himself exactly where he wanted to be and that wasn't in the lower echelons of the fraud division of the FBI.

"You'll be a GS-12 but Elliot will keep you comfortable. He's got other accounts to pay you."

"What about you? What are you doing here? I mean why not just meet me in the city, at headquarters? Why am I not meeting Elliot?"

"Pfft," the old man snorted, "that gossip mill? It leaks like a sieve. No, if you want a secret known, tell one of your coworkers; if you want to keep a secret, tell *no one*. The files I gave you this morning are for your cover operation for the agency. It's your red herring, see? That cover operation pays for everything we do here."

Michael nodded his head, but he had no idea what the old man was talking about.

The old man drummed his fingers on a folder, "This is the real deal. But now with all this new technology, I'm falling behind." He shrugged, "I can't keep up. I'm from the analogue age." The old man shook his head in frustration, "And I've been thwarting these assholes for 15 years. But it's a whole new ballgame, new players with new toys. "

"Fifteen years? And you haven't caught them? No arrests?"

The old man looked at Michael in astonishment, but then grinned and nodded his head. He looked down at the papers, cleared his throat and said quietly, "There are no arrests, Michael. This is not a thing, a tort, that goes into a *court of law*."

Michael watched the old man get up and patiently pour them cups of coffee, "Let me explain from the beginning."

M. Saylor Billings

CHAPTER 1

JULY 2006

"I am so lost!"

Lorna Tollison snatched the chirping cell phone off the passenger seat of her rented sedan and wailed into it, "I am so lost!"

"Where are you?" Sally Thompson, Lorna's partner, asked patiently.

"Dude, if I knew that I wouldn't be lost."

"Look for a road sign." Sally continued in a well-modulated tone.

"I just past a giant Styrofoam watermelon on the side of the road."

Sally paused. "When you left the airport did you turn right or left?"

"Okay, here's what happened," Lorna began as she continued to cruise with the morning traffic down the crowded two lane road.

Sally listened to the circular explanation of why Lorna

had had to turn left coming out of the Oakland Airport rental car lot and not right to get on the highway. Sitting at her desk in Manhattan, she stared at her computer screen, following Lorna's progress on Google maps. Lorna had three days and four thousand dollars in cash to find a place to live. Sally had coined it an epic "bicoastal three-days to find a place to live" quest when she handed Lorna the sweaty wad of cash before the flight out of JFK airport. It would be a race against time. They had contacted a real estate rental agent in the Hayes Valley district in San Francisco and put together rental packets that consisted of credit reports, prior rental agreements and landlord recommendation letters, Lorna's tax return from last year and Sally's employment agreement from the U.S. Housing and Urban Development Administration – they had left nothing to chance. What could possibly go wrong?

"I just need a street name and I can help you." Sally persisted.

Lorna ended the call and flopped the cell phone onto the passenger seat in frustration,

"There are no fucking street signs!" She yelled at the windshield. Her eyes burned, her neck hurt, and she was in dire, dire need of coffee. She crossed over a bridge and into a well-manicured neighborhood. She saw a green sign that read OAKLAND in white lettering with an arrow pointing ahead and took a deep relaxing breath. She followed the road around past another bridge on her right. There was no sign for Oakland near the bridge so she continued straight on. Finally she saw another sign for Oakland and went through a tunnel that dropped her off in Oakland's Chinatown. Sitting at a stoplight, she pressed the number 2 and speed dialed Sally back.

"Do you know where you are now?" Sally asked.

"Not yet, but I'm in Oakland, I think. I'm at 7th and Jefferson." Lorna answered.

"Okay." Sally quickly scanned her computer screen and

enlarged the map, "Okay, go right on..."

"Hang on – let me pull over," Lorna interrupted. She pulled her car over to the side and backed into the open space before continuing. "Go ahead."

"Well, you need to be on Warner and that will lead you to 880 North which leads to the Bay Bridge." Sally blurted out in one breath.

Lorna looked around, "Warner then 880 North. How many streets over do I go from here?"

"Two, it's Jefferson, then Warner."

"Okay let me call you back when I'm on 880."

"Drive safely, you're tired, honey. Why don't you go to a hotel first?"

"Yes, of course, but don't you think I should find San Francisco first?"

They hung up and Lorna pulled back out into the morning traffic. After Jefferson was Warner. She turned left which led her through another tunnel that led her to a wide-open area, different from where she went through the tunnel the first time. She pulled the car over to a convenience store and went inside.

"Excuse me, could you point me to 880 North?" She asked the man at the counter.

He smiled and shrugged.

Lorna looked around, "Um, direct-see-own-ess? Ocho ocho, um zero?" She moved her fingers signing the numbers out.

He smiled and shook his head at her.

"Okay, parlez vous francais?" She tried again.

He shook his head.

"Sprechen Sie Deutsch, bitte?" She wasn't giving up.

He stared at her.

She thought about what Sally had taught her, "Jo sun. Um okay bah, bah – and I don't know how to say zero in the Chinese."

He was being amused now.

Lorna dropped her shoulders. "So you're just not going to make any effort here, huh? Nothing." Lorna smiled and shook her head back at him. "But you *work* in a public store. Unbelievable. Not even a yes or no or I don't know?"

The man smiled, shrugged at her. He picked up a candy bar off the counter and let it drop and waved his arms around.

"Well, asshole, I'm not going to buy your shitty candy. You understand *that* I bet." Lorna stormed out of the store and got back in the car.

Driving further she found the entrance to the tunnel again and went back through, her eyes darting around for a sign. She turned right out of the tunnel and saw the overpass ahead but no entrance.

"I'm in hell." She said aloud. "The plane never landed. I'm in a special kind of hell. Travelers' hell." She drove past the convenience store to a stop-light and called Sally.

"I'm just so ungodly lost." She whispered into the phone, choking back tears.

"Give me a street name, I've got the maps opened."

The light turned green and Lorna proceeded ahead with the other cars, "Warner."

"Okay, Chinatown?"

"NO. I just came from Chinatown. I went through a tunnel. Wait, there's a Starbucks – let me pull over and I'll call you back." Lorna flopped the cell phone down into the seat next to her and turned right into the parking lot.

She put her face in her hands and rubbed her eyes. She had been up now for forty-eight hours and the last nine had not gone as planned or imagined. Her six a.m. flight from JFK to Oakland airport meant that she was up and out of their Manhattan apartment by three a.m., which wouldn't have been a problem except that their six-month old boy kittens had reached the age of testosterone-fueled nighttime fighting and the mewing had thwarted her sleep. The flight, which should have been a five-hour cross-country nap, was instead a baby-screaming match, coupled with an elderly woman next to her who insisted on having a conversation about how she would handle the screaming babies, every 20 minutes. But she was here now or somewhere, at least. She got out of the car, went into the bustling Starbucks and ordered a coffee.

"Thank you," said Lorna as she took her black coffee off the counter and caught the barista's eye, "and could you tell me the name of this city?"

"Ohlone." The barista smiled.

"Thanks." Lorna took her cup of coffee back out to the car and speed dialed Sally.

"Your on Oh-Loan Island." Sally said triumphantly.

"Yeah, it's pronounced Ah-lawn-ee." Lorna said.

"It's an island."

"That would explain the tunnels and bridges."

"Get back on Warner and stay in the right lane and follow it through Chinatown till it circles around, kinda, and that will dump you onto 880, but it's like a full circle." Sally was staring at the Google Maps on her computer screen. She could see how this could be very confusing for Lorna. Ohlone Island lay parallel between Oakland and San Francisco, and Lorna had never been to this part of the country.

"Will you see if there are any diners around here? I'm getting peckish."

"Hang on." Sally opened another page on her computer and typed in: Diners Ohlone. "You'll have to drive to the other side of the island."

"How far?" Lorna asked.

"Hang on." Sally typed in the diner's address on the maps page. "Two miles. But you could totally just go to a hotel and take a nap and a shower. You'd feel so much better."

"I know and I will. I just yelled at a brown person for not being able to speak English. I'm a frust-racist." Lorna confessed. "Will you call the realtors and let them know I'm going to be late?"

"Yes. Go eat some racist breakfast and calm down. You have plenty of time still. Call me when you check in somewhere. I knew we should have done this together. I'm sorry."

"No." Lorna stopped her. "We've got a plan – we just need to stick to it. It's a bump, that's all, and I'm just tired. I'll call you in a bit."

"The diner is called Trident Diner off of Colony. Turn right out of the Starbucks parking lot onto Colony and go straight."

"Got it, thanks honey."

They hung up again and Lorna started off out of the parking lot onto Colony.

The diner was filled with people, so Lorna took a seat at the counter and had her breakfast. She left feeling calmer and focused again. She stood outside the diner and checked her watch. It was only 9:15 am. The street traffic was still heavy, which meant it would still be heavy on the highway leading into San Francisco, she reasoned. She saw a group of people power walking down the sidewalk and smiled. A quick brisk walk around the block was a good idea after sitting up all night and it would only take a minute. The move from New York City had been their first big decision together, a chance to take a break from the hectic and chaotic city life. New York would always be there and they could always go back some day. After some debate about where in the country to move, Sally had put in for a transfer to San Francisco. Lorna had never been there but Sally had visited a few times in her life. It would be an adventure for them. The opening for a position in the San Francisco office came within weeks. They hadn't counted on that. Sally was to report to the Federal Housing Office in San Francisco in one month's time. So, the scramble to pack up their lives, say goodbye to friends and colleagues, and the move across country began.

Half way around the block, Lorna turned right onto Center Street. Time stood still and her mouth fell open. It was storybook perfect! Down the wide stretched avenue, Coastal Live Oaks stood as sentinels in front of manicured lawns and colorful Victorian homes that stretch into the sky. She had just left a typical July in New York, which meant stifling humidity, urine soaked subway stairs, blasting air conditioning at sub-artic levels and wilting plants. But here, everything was in bloom. Colorful rose bushes in true English gardens sat behind white picket fences gleaming in the sunbeams, without a hint of irony. She looked up at the trees where sunlight was beaming through the leaves. "Duuuuuude. It's like fucking Ginger Bread Lane."

The beauty drew her in and she strolled down Center Street, decompressing and absorbing the ambiance. A craftsman bungalow had a small wooden sign out from that read ISLAND REALTORS. Lorna turned up the path, lined with fragrant lavender bushes, which led to the front door.

Upon entering, the heavy waft of rose smacked Lorna across the forehead, she blinked involuntarily several times, swallowed and rubbed her nose. A well-coifed elderly lady sat at one of the six desks that lined what would have once been the living room and smiled.

"Hello," she greeted, in what Lorna thought was a remarkably young voice.

"Hello," Lorna smiled her, "My name is Lorna Tollison, I'm moving out here from New York City and I've taken a completely wrong turn somewhere –

"Oh then, welcome to our island. You're on the City Island of Ohlone. Would you like a map?"

"I would, thank you." Lorna answered gratefully as the lady picked up some papers from a three-stack tray and handed them to her.

"You'll come back and let me know if I can be of service to you?" The elderly lady smiled shuffling Lorna out of the front door.

"Yes, of course." Lorna took the papers and scrambled back to the car.

She pressed the number 2 on her cell phone, speed-dialing Sally, and backed out of the parking lot.

"Where are you?" Sally asked.

"It's really beautiful here. I mean it's definitely a suburb." She continued driving slowly on Center Street gazing at the homes. "I've never seen anything like this, Sally. I think this is just the change we're looking for."

"And you are where?"

"I'm still on Ohlone."

"Honey, you have a 10 a.m. appointment in San Francisco." Sally chided.

"No Sally, *this* is it. We said we wanted a change well, *this,* is a big change. No urine soaked subways, no humidity. Dude, it smells like *happy*."

"What are you seeing?" Sally was curious as she typed the words Ohlone Island into the Craig's List search engine.

"You know the beginning of musical movies that are set in the 1930's, and they have the long opening pan of the streets in an idyllic little town with children on bikes and people strolling? All of a sudden people tap dance out of their homes and begin the opening number? I found where they shoot those scenes!"

"I don't think I saw that one. But that's fine. It's hard to believe that really exists."

"I'll take pictures."

"Where are you now?"

Lorna looked around and pulled the car over to the side of the road. "I think I'm in their downtown," she looked at the street signs, "I'm on the corner of Center Street and High Street."

Sally switched sites back to the map site, "So you're at Center and their High street. What's the name of it?"

"Listen, High. Like, I can reach this *high*."

Sally paused and enlarged the street map. "Their high street is called High Street and the Center Street runs down the middle of the island, convenient. I thought you meant their main street."

Lorna moved the receiver down and made a silent scream and rubbed her forehead.

"Are you silent screaming?"

"No."

"Well get some paper out – there's a bunch of rental addresses to give you."

"I want to find the Chamber of Commerce – they always have maps and info about the town."

"Yeah but take these down first and you can get a better feel for them when you go to the Chamber."

By three o'clock in the afternoon Lorna was feeling the weight of the day. The adrenaline she'd felt in the morning hours was wearing off. She had managed to drive by or stop into fifteen separate apartment complexes, dwellings, and loft spaces from the lists that Sally and the lady from the Chamber of Commerce gave her. Nothing seemed right yet, but there were a couple of possibilities. She was tired and wanted to find a hotel and rest. She pulled the car over to the side, leaned the seat back, took a deep breath and rested her eyes for a moment. She knew she had to push forward. What should she do next? She opened her eyes again and pulled out her notebook and began calling more phone numbers to make walk-through appointments for the next day. She was only able to reach three of the people on the list and felt a little uncomfortable at her lack of choices. She drove back to where she had seen a copy store and made three more copies of the rental packets. Back in the car, she leaned the seat back and rested her eyes again. Just keep moving forward, she thought again, what next? She pulled off the money belt she was wearing that held the four thousand dollars and rubbed her waist. Living in New York City had taught Sally that nothing says yes like cold cash when you want to make a quick transaction. Her cell phone rang again.

"Hi, Honey." Lorna laid her head back on the seat rest.

"How's it going?"

"I made a few appointments – nothing like I wanted, though."

"Something just popped up on Craig's List. It's on Saint Charles Place. It looks really cute."

"Oh," Lorna leaned up and looked around. "I'm near there, I think."

"Where are you?" Sally asked switching back over to the map screen.

Lorna looked for street signs. "I'm at Copy Cat's on the corner of Belk and Linden."

Sally enlarged the screen again, "Okay three blocks north, toward that military base. It's on your left. The big yellow house."

Lorna turned the ignition key. "I'm on it."

Moments later Lorna looked up through the windshield at the yellow high peaked Colonial Revival with a round turret. "Oh, you beauty! I found you."

A young woman with long sun-streaked hair in a t-shirt and worn, low-hanging jeans stepped out onto the front porch and lit a cigarette. Lorna hopped out of the car and eagerly approached her.

"Hi." Lorna smiled.

"Hi." The young woman gave the disheveled dishwater blonde's athletic build a quick once over.

"I'm completely intruding, my name is Lorna Tollison, and this property just came up on Craig's List. I live in New York and I only have two days to find a place to live here. Are you the owner?"

The young woman looked out across the street, "That was fast! She just called them this morning. My mom rents the place. Shannon and Stan own it. They live in Washington State."

"Would it be too much to ask if I looked around? I'm so sorry to be pushy, I promise I'm not a weirdo or anything. I just have so very little time." Lorna pleaded with the girl.

"The place is kind of a mess, I was getting ready to clean it."

"I won't judge. I'll clean the toilet for you if you'll help me. I'm that desperate."

The young woman smiled and nodded, "Come on. I'm Carol by the way." She opened the screen door for Lorna to enter. The expansive rooms were highlighted with hand crafted redwood panel around the sideboards, doors, and windows. The fireplace had a hand carved redwood mantle that made Lorna gasp a little.

As they took the cursory tour, Carol explained, "The washer and dryer are in the basement. And you should know that comes out of your hot water heater." She made a pinched frown and raised an eyebrow. "The garage is out back." She led Lorna through the kitchen to the back door.

"What are the owners like?" Lorna asked as they walked into the back yard.

"Let's just say when they're in town, I make myself scarce. They're not bad, just different." Carol concluded.

Different? Lorna thought. Different is a deep and vast canyon that covers anything from not eating eggs to chanting in tongues while wearing tin foil hats – different. Lorna stopped staring into the back yard and realized she was at the end of her tour, "It's a nice big yard. Thank you so much."

"No problem, I need the karma. Good luck." Carol turned and went back toward the back door as Lorna made her way down the driveway.

"Luck, my ass." Lorna muttered to herself patting her waist where the money belt *had* been. Her heart raced and she practically ran back to the car and quickly scanned the interior until she saw the money belt on the floorboard.

Lorna settled back into the car, wrapping the money belt back around her waist, and called Sally.

"Well?" Sally asked anxiously.

"This is it! Call the owners or give me the number. If they can meet me tonight, it'd be great. I have everything with me." Lorna looked about the car again for the rental folders.

"...11 a.m." Sally was saying.

"I'm sorry what?"

"They're having an open house tomorrow at 11 a.m."

"Shit." Lorna cupped her forehead in her hand. "Competition."

"I know."

"Can you call them anyway? Ask them what they need to secure the place and we'll make a plan from there." Lorna asked.

"Well, you saw the place right?" Sally had already formulated a plan.

"Yeah, the daughter took me through everything."

"Then while everyone else is walking through, you pull the owners aside and give them the packet with the money in it. It's plenty to cover the deposits and first months rent. Just get your stuff in first and the cash. Mainly the cash, okay?"

"Okay."

"You're sure this is the one?"

"It's the best I've seen yet." Lorna confirmed.

"Then take the leap. I trust your judgment." Sally nodded to herself.

"Really? Cause I feel like I might have impaired judgment at this point."

Sally was looking at the Google map image of the house. It did look ideal. "No, you're right. It's a good call." Sally reassured her.

At 4:30 Lorna maneuvered her rented sedan in front of The Coffee Klatch and entered the small brick framed building. She was hungry but felt she needed a decaf coffee and to just sit somewhere other than the car and process her day first. At the front counter she ordered her decaf and a buttery croissant. She looked around the cafe; heads bowed over laptops occupied every table. As she scanned the room, she quickly made a list of reasons as to why a coffee house would be so crowded at 4:30 in the afternoon. Were they students, unemployed, hackers, or is it nerd-mating season? She finally spied an open seat at a table with a woman who was about her age.

"Pardon me, may I sit here?" Lorna asked the woman. The woman looked around first and then at Lorna. Lorna was still wearing the clothes she'd left New York in, black summer sweater, blue jeans and black loafers. Her pony tail that only half way held her long blonde hair was cocked sideways on the back of her head. The resulting wayward strands of hair created a halo effect.

"Sure." The woman lurched her head back down to the laptop.

Lorna had neglected to bring her maps and materials with her and adjusted the money belt as she sat down. She looked around - youngish, middle-class ... most of them were wearing outdoor type of clothes. Lorna smiled to herself. In Manhattan, you dress camera ready, but here, you dress spin class or mountain climbing ready. Very casual, she thought, don't these people have jobs to go to? Maybe she was in a college hangout and didn't know it. She took a sip of coffee and rubbed her forehead with her hand before opening her croissant bag. One by one people were looking up from their glowing laptops and glaring at her. She turned to the woman across the table.

"My name is Lorna." The man at the next table to the right looked up and smiled at Lorna. Lorna looked at the top of her tablemate's head and stretched her arm out next to the laptop keyboard. The woman looked up startled.

"Hi, my name is Lorna." Lorna smiled at the woman's startled look. "I'm from Manhattan and I'm hoping to move here. Could you tell me a little about the island?"

"Oh," the woman smiled, in what Lorna thought was relief, "well let's see, at the north end is the old military base. The Navy closed it down in the 1990's. There are two main drags that lead into Oakland, High street at the south end, and Warner at the north end. Um, South Shore has an outdoor mall; near Warner is the port where there are more shops and a business park. And everything in between is houses, churches, schools and neighborhood-y type things. Parks."

An older man with a Sean Connery hairpiece, circa "The Hunt for Red October," at the next table left piped in, "there is a hospital near South Shore. But you can't be born or buried on the island," before he bowed his head back down and focused on an area map.

Aha! A paper map indeed! Lorna thought.

"You look like a soccer mom." He mumbled aloud while looking down at his map.

Lorna blinked at the woman across from her who had heard him and was smiling nervously.

Leaning over to him Lorna said softly, "Sean Connery called, he wants his wig back." She turned back to her tablemate and added reassuringly, "Well, it's lovely."

"And quite. Lots of children. It's mainly a transit community. Most people work in San Francisco."

"And *trans* back and forth into the city?" Lorna asked.

"Yes there is a lot of trans-ing done here." Lorna's tablemate joined the joke.

"What are all of these people doing here in the middle of the day?" Lorna asked.

"Working."

"On what?"

"No," the woman explained, "they're like, at work. They're working on-line."

Lorna looked around wide eyed as the woman continued, "Silicon Valley is only about 50 miles away. They're trying to label the island Silicon Island."

"Oh I see," Lorna said brightly and then pronounced to the room, "my people! I have come home!" Sean Connery's hairpiece chuckled to himself. Lorna's tablemate's eyes jutted about nervously as Lorna continued, "I was lost and now I am found." She turned to her tablemate and began energetically, "Okay so I flew out here yesterday, well on the red eye, so this morning. I've never heard of this place, I got lost on my way to San Francisco and wound up here. I think I found a place to live already. I work online too. I write content for magazines and websites. This is weird isn't it?"

The woman smiled and nodded understandingly, "You must be exhausted."

"I am!" Lorna agreed. "And I think I'm having an allergic reaction to something making my forehead itch!"

"You don't sound like a New Yorker – your accent." Her tablemate frowned and shook her head.

"It's a dialect. You speak with a dialect and you accent parts of words or accent a *word*. I grew up in Atlanta."

"You don't sound like that either." The woman said.

"Trust me," Lorna said conspiratorially, "you move from Atlanta to New York you lose that shit fast. If you want to be taken seriously."

"I see." Her tablemate took this as good wisdom.

Lorna was ebullient again, "Anyway, my partner is in New York and was telling me by cell phone places to go that were on Craig's List and I think we found a place. I'm totally exhausted, but I feel really good about this."

Lorna's excitement was infectious. Sean Connery's hairpiece looked up and nodded, "Right on."

Lorna nodded back at him, "Everything is just falling into place."

"Well," the woman smiled warming up to Lorna. "Congratulations, you made it to Gayberry."

"What?" Lorna asked unsure of whether or not to be offended.

"Some people call this Gayberry, because of all the gay

families. I'm Annie, by the way."

"Thanks, Annie. Can I get you a coffee or something? I'm sorry I've imposed on you. Is there a hotel near by? I think I need to crash. My ears have started ringing." Lorna rubbed her forehead again, which had turned a bright red.

Annie closed her laptop and smiled at the weary traveler, "Well there are two I'd recommend –"

"Let me guess, one at the south end and one at the north?" Lorna interrupted.

"You're getting the picture."

"Well I found an apartment in a yellow Victorian and they're having an open house that I need to get to early tomorrow." Said Lorna.
"Where is it?" Annie asked.

"On Saint Charles Place."

"I know it." Annie said excitedly, "Across from the senior center?"

"I don't know … senior center?"

"The pink building?"

"Oh yes," Lorna remembered.

"I live across Liberty on Saint Charles. We'd be catty corner to each other." Annie took a paper napkin and wrote a pencil-drawing map to show Lorna, "The O Line runs down Liberty here and into San Francisco. It's great if you take public transit. My husband takes it when he works in the city."

"How long have you lived here?"

"Two years," Annie answered, "my husband and I moved up from San Jose. He's in Human Resources."

"Well my partner is an attorney for the Fed, so she'll probably take the O Line. If it's that convenient."

"It is." Annie said.

"I'm sorry." Sean Connery's hairpiece turned to the two women and spoke softly. "I couldn't help but overhear your conversation. I'm glad you found the island. I think you'll be very happy here after New York."

"Well, thank you." Lorna smiled.

"And here." The old man took out his keys and fiddled with them pulling off an ornate barrel shaped skeleton key about the length of his thumb. "I found this decades ago in an old sea captain's house that was being torn down." He handed the key to Lorna. "A welcome present."

Lorna took the key, "Oh, it's heavy. Thank you. That's very nice. Maybe it goes to a sunken sea treasure chest."

"You never know."

Annie watched this exchange and said, "Why don't I show you around and some good places for you to have dinner before you crash?" Annie offered.

"Oh that'd be so nice but I've intruded so much … you were working so diligently."

"It's no problem." Annie offered again with a shrug.

"Really? Only if you're sure." Maybe it was exhaustion, or the fresh clean air, or fate, but Lorna could not believe her good fortune.

"Do you have a car?" Annie asked.

"Yes, it's out front." Lorna answered as Annie began to pack up her laptop.

"Well, when I moved here I really could have used a drive-around by a friendly neighbor. So let me do this, I need the karma."

"Karma's big here, huh?" It was the second time Lorna had heard that today.

"It's as real as God is here." Annie said as she moved toward the front door.

CHAPTER 2

SEPTEMBER 2007

"The coldest winter I ever spent was summer in San Francisco."
~Author Unknown

The weather had been steadily warming up over the past week. And that was perplexing to Lorna. The Bay Area has so many microclimates she had been unable to pin point a weather pattern, let alone any actual season at any given time of year. But there were a lot of things about the island that Lorna had found perplexing in the last year. There were 68 dental practices on the island. *68, in 11 square miles.* And 83 nail salons. They were everywhere ... but that wasn't it. No, there was something deeper at play here. Something under the surface that she couldn't quite put her finger on. And it scratched at her brain, needling her to uncover whatever *it* was. There was something invisible *because* - that thing, that *it* - was so obvious. Whatever *it* was it was hiding in plain sight.

But she caught it in her periphery every now and again like a ghost.

The daily excitement of their adventure, living in completely new surroundings, was wearing off. Lorna was starting to feel hermetically sealed in a 60 degree suburb cut off from the daily bustle and socialization of city life. If pressed she would admit she missed New York City, but only if pressed. In New York she had rented a small office in the east village with three other writers, the "office rats," all of whom annoyed one another yet each respected the office rules. It had been a place to get work accomplished. The apartment's circular turret room was now her office; in the beginning the solitude was a blessing.

But one day, about nine months after their move, Sally came home from work to find Lorna in her office still in her pajamas. The next day she came home to find the same thing *and* Lorna was still in the same set of pajamas. This was not like Lorna, who was fairly fastidious about her appearance and liked routine, so Sally took it as a red flag.

"Do you feel – " Sally stopped. She should have thought this through first.

"What?"

"Are you okay? Are you sick?" Sally asked, taking the concerned route.

"Yeah. No. Why?"

"Well, um, honey, I was just thinking. Maybe you'd like a hot bath?"

Lorna stared at Sally for a beat and then smiled. "I'm disgusting aren't I?"

"Well, no, I just think you've been working so hard the past couple of days."

"No I haven't." Lorna shrugged, correcting her. "Same shit, different day."

Sally took Lorna into her arms and pulled her close, "Okay, look, you haven't bathed or brushed your teeth for three days now. And I don't believe you've left the house in five. Am I right?"

Lorna nodded.

"It's a slippery slope. One I don't think you would consciously put yourself on."

"What are you saying?"

Sally walked Lorna over to a framed photo of the two of them at one of Lorna's fellow office rats book party in New York; they had both worked all day, gone to an early dinner, off to a Ranger's game, then to the party. Yet Lorna looked radiant in the photo.

"Now, come with me," Sally walked Lorna into the bathroom and faced a mirror arranging Lorna and herself in the same pose. "Okay, what's different about *this* picture?"

"Wow, you've gained weight!" Lorna pointed at their reflections.

Sally nodded smiling, "Touché."

"And that chick next to you is a hot mess!" Lorna pointed at her own reflection.

Sally was right of course, and since that evening intervention Lorna developed a routine; she would get up, stretch, have breakfast, shower and put on fresh clothes. She would go out to the street and take the O Line bus to another part of the island, pick up a croissant or morning muffin and ride the bus back to settle in for her workday. Sometimes she would work a little at the coffee shop hoping to find future office mates, but she just as often found the coffee shops crowded with deeply unsocial people staring at laptops. Yet another thing she found perplexing about this area – the coffee house crowd. But for now this routine seemed to be working. While it did not delineate her work and home space, it differentiated time for her.

Lorna stared out of the window of her office, past the lemon tree to the Pink Senior Center – which Lorna suddenly noted had recently been painted from pink to blue. Why? That must be confusing to people, especially the elderly, she reckoned. Today she was to write an article for online publications about what to wear when traveling in Northern California. The article would be published under the pseudonym "Rebecca Charles" and then rewritten under a male pseudonym "Robert Cook" for an online men's magazine.

Lorna had come to have five pseudonyms under one banner, *Drug Store Publishers,* by accident. When she began her career, like every other writer who comes to New York, she couldn't get published. So, on a whim, she wrote a humorous but informative article about a man's relationship with his socks under the byline Robert Cook and sent it to a prominent men's magazine. It was her first article ever published, and Robert, with his irreverent look at all things ordinary, became the go-to guy for several publications. The problem was she couldn't cash his checks. So Lorna opened Drug Store Publishers and that grew into four other pseudonyms, as well as her real byline. Each name had its own style and personality. Writing any article under Rebecca's byline, however, is always difficult for Lorna because "Rebecca Style" always uses the latest idioms, has no sense of irony, and is vapid. Lorna stared at the blinking curser on the computer monitor, "Are you mocking me?"

She pulled out a fresh sheet of paper from the printer and wrote by hand.

> *It really bothers me that they painted the Pink Senior Center blue. It's rude. If it was so- named because of some benefactors, say a Mr. and Mrs. Pink, then it is an affront to their legacy. If it was called so because the building was originally painted pink, then it is confusing for the elderly and that's just cruel. If it was named Pink because it was originally for homosexuals, then that's fucked up — what happened there? Did an angry mob of the elderly attack the homosexuals with adult diapers*

and take over the center? It makes no sense. Unless of course if the original owners were socialists. You know what else doesn't make sense? The majority of people on this island, elderly and young alike, are very liberal leaning. Practically socialists. Yet there is practically no middle class here. But it is a paradise, no less; nice well-kept public amenities like tennis courts, pools, parks, golf course, and beaches. And why, in the name of all that is holy, is the only fine dining steak house hidden away on a side street surrounded by crumbling warehouses with no parking anywhere near it?

Lorna put her pencil down. The Rebecca writing style was just not coming out of her brain today. She dropped her arms to her side as she craned her neck back, letting gravity pull down on the weight of her head between her shoulder blades. Lifting her bottom lip up to close her mouth she dropped it open again with a, "baaahhh" sound. It felt good, so she did it again. And once again, but lifting her head back up, letting the sound rotate down as the nasally sound became more of a growl. She watched some elderly people gather around the side entrance of the Pink Senior Center. Her mother would have been about that age now…. going on a group outing on the Charter Bus, maybe to a casino.

She was getting to the root of her problem now. There was an anniversary coming up, one she didn't relish but would have to acknowledge. At age 32, Lorna was older than her mother had been when her mother died. As horrible and shocking as the sudden terminal cancer had been for her parents, they had taken Lorna, when was 12 years old at the time, through a rehearsal funeral to mitigate what emotional shock they could. She remembered her mother standing next to an open casket saying, "And I'll be lying here and I'll have my arms crossed on my chest like this. What do you think about that Lorna?" Her parents, Quill and Lynn, were strange that way. Never fighting, always prepared, emotionally honest and quirky people. Lynn had taught people who were losing their sight to be blind before the fact. Lynn not only taught them the mechanics of being blind but also taught them the emotional levity that she believed was necessary for living with that disability. But it was Quill's idea to have "Blind Parties" for adult students that included guessing games like "Guess which finger I'm holding up" and "Guess what alcohol I'm drinking." And the students in turn were dedicated to Lynn, never alerting the school to their semi-annual parties.

One of Lynn's younger students, Tessa, had been a clever and gregarious girl with wild curly red hair. Tessa had a progressive congenital disorder that was causing her to lose her vision from the center of her gaze, progressing outward into her peripheral vision, resulting, over time, in complete blindness. Tessa's family had used the insurance money she had received to prepare her for a lifetime of blindness for a brand new shiny car, because how else would they be able to tote around a blind girl? So Tessa, 14 years old and facing a lifetime of blindness, did the only thing she could do – she offered to barter for Lynn's time. Mainly, she babysat Lorna, who was enamored with Tessa's hair and the older girl's friendship, but Tessa also acted as Lynn's assistant at the school. Yet, it was Quill who took a particular shine to this girl he named "Hey Kid". He thought she was a natural engineer, which was his own passion and career, and believed she was capable of great things. So after Tessa's parents were convicted of vehicular manslaughter, there was no question where Tessa would live and who would eventually adopt her.

In the end, Lynn had considered herself lucky to have the time to prepare her family for her departure with letters and instructions to them all. And in honor of their matriarch, her brood followed all her instructions and advice. They were all the better for it. For years after her mother's death, Lorna had thought her father to be an avid bowler, with a weekly game night. It wasn't until Lorna was 18 that Tessa told her he had been going to grief counseling and later had been in the company of women his own age. Following his wife's instructions, Quill was careful not to bring these women home until Lorna left for college, not because it was unfair to his daughters but because it would have been unfair to the other women.

Lorna was actually the first person to bring a date home, and to no one's surprise the date's name was Jennifer. Quill had cried, not because of the date, because it was another one of Lynn's predictions that came true, and it made him miss her even more.

After college Lorna struck off for New York City where, after several years of dating and living *la vida loca* single life, she met Sally. Lorna had been working on an article about a recent investigation into HUD activities and Sally was a federal attorney for the Department of Housing that Lorna wanted to interview about the case.

Sally, a tall brunette with wavy black hair and big round brown eyes, did not bear the hallmarks of her Asian ancestry. When Sally revealed her "hoppa" roots to Lorna, Lorna responded with, "Are you sure? You look more Eastern European."

"Yes," Sally responded, "my father was Portuguese and English and my mom was full Han Chinese. But this look did help me when I did relief work in Bosnia after college."

Lorna stared out of the office window with unseeing eyes. She was picturing Sally, wrapped up in her camel wool overcoat with the collar up around a black scarf, strolling toward her on 5th Avenue in New York City. A car horn blared outside and snapped Lorna out of her gaze and she began typing again:

Like most days on the Island it's about 5

> *degrees cooler than comfortable. Plus sized males must love it, but for the rest of us it just means wearing another layer. That's the first thing you learn about moving to the Northern California Coast -- it's all about the layers. Forget what you heard about sun and surf and wind up a colorful scarf around your neck —*

She deleted what she wrote with a tart reprimand to herself, "Come on Rebecca if you can't say anything nice, shut the hell up," and started again:

> *Remember the lyrics from The Lady is a Tramp? "She's hates California, it's cold and it's damp." Well a lot of the time it is, but for the savvy dresser —*

She stopped typing again and looked over at Patience and Fortitude, their yellow tabbies, who stretched and yawned in a synchronized way after she asked them, "Why can't I write today?" She sighed and looked around her office for a distraction and picked up the phone and speed dialed 2 — Sally's office phone number.

"This is Sally."

"Hi. Did you make it to the gyno?" Lorna asked.

"Yes, I did. She said that it wasn't necessary to come back for a couple of years. That I had three years of screening and not to worry about it again until I'm forty."

"Pfft, what does she know?" Lorna snorted. Because of her mother's aggressive cancer, Lorna insisted on yearly cancer screenings for everyone in the family. She would say, "Why play with fire?" -- despite the fact that it was actually only Lorna who could be genetically affected by her mother's cancer.

"What's going on?" Sally asked, not wanting to get Lorna revved up on this topic again.

"Nothing. Anything exciting happen on the O Line this

morning?"

"Are you still working on that fashion article?"

"No. Yes."

"That bad?" Sally sympathized.

Lorna grunted.

"Why do you insist on taking these assignments?"

"Money."

"You're going to have to start weighing the effort against the pay on these things. Is it worth it?" Sally explained.

Lorna paused. "Didn't you tell me that if I didn't do it I would just be leaving money on the table?"

"Did I say that?"

"Yes, Counselor, you did." Lorna said accusingly.

Sally glanced at her calendar; it was about that time of year when Lorna went into a mourning funk for a few days. "Okay, we can figure this out. Whose voice is it in?" She said in a calmer tone.

"Rebecca."

"Oh God. I thought you were going to retire her?" Sally couldn't hide her disgust for the ebullient Rebecca Style. "I hate her."

"I know but the editor wanted a style slash fashion article for spring in separate travel sections, I have to do it in Bob's voice for the men's articles too. And who better to write it?"

"Bob?" Sally asked.

"Robert." Lorna corrected herself.

"No, you're right it has to be Rebecca's style. Just please, don't use the word 'juicy'." Sally pleaded.

"No. Right. Descriptive words are hard, but no I won't use the word 'juicy' nor 'journey'."

"Why don't you get some input?"

"Input" was Lorna's word for research before she wrote an article. However, according to Lorna, "input" could also be going to the movies, shopping, baking, reading gossip tabloids, exercise, or eating vast quantities of chocolate.

"Like what? Go shopping?" Lorna smiled at the

thought.

"No. Well, if you want to, I need some black socks."

"Oh I know, I'll go up to High Street and look in on that Ohlone Museum." Lorna's voice brightened.

"I thought you said it looked like an absurdist garage sale?"

"It does, but I'm curious, and they have that chair I want to look at again before the antiques fair in San Jose this weekend."

"And…?" Sally wasn't buying Lorna's explanation.

"And – I feel sorry for them."

"You feel sorry," Sally began slowly, "for a museum."

"Well okay, here's what happened: In the year that we've been here, they've had flood, and a fire, and I just read they were losing their funding from the city. And all they want is a little local pride. A place in history, y' know?"

"But there's the USS Hornet." Sally countered.

"That's the military; it has nothing to do with what came before the military came in and left a toxic mess, or with local flavor."

"Okay," Sally changed the subject, "what's for dinner?"

"Pork Chops."

"Grilled?" Sally hoped aloud.

"It's going to be cold tonight I think."

"Grilled?" Sally pressed it.

"Yes." Lorna acquiesced.

"See you tonight at 6:30, Sweetheart."

"Okay, bye."

Sally hung up her phone and drummed her fingers on the receiver. There had to be a way to get Lorna to call her cell phone and not her office phone. It must be casual, she thought to herself, imagining what she wanted the conversation to be like, even off-handed. Over dinner she'd mention that she had missed an important call. Lorna would ask, "But what about the various phone lines – wouldn't it just roll over to another line?" "No," she would answer, "those federal lines are archaic." She must be completely plausible when explaining.

Sally mindlessly lifted up a sheet of paper and touched her cell phone. Her mind wandered ... how could she make it Lorna's idea? *That* would surely work. Maybe she should just mention to Lorna about the memo she had received reminding everyone that their phone calls are sometimes recorded. At the moment she began tapping her cell phone it sprung to life. Sally shot straight up out of her seat and back down again. She snatched up the phone and pressed the answer button while bringing it to her ear in one fluid movement. She quickly brought it back down to see the name and number on the screen, which read "Tessa," before saying hello.

"Hi Darlin'!" Tessa, although adept at all things technical, hasn't mastered the idea that she doesn't have to scream into her cell phone to be heard. Sally frantically clicked down the volume button before Tessa yelled, "How are ya' doin'!"

"Good – how about you?"

Tessa went on. "Have you gotten all the kinks worked out of your lunch schedule yet?"

White-hot worry singed though Sally. It would be just like Tessa to fly all the way from Atlanta and be sitting in a cab out front of her San Francisco office ready to take Sally to lunch. "Oh God" Sally muttered unconsciously.

"Is Lorna making you take your lunch?"

"No," said Sally, "I just remembered something, I'm supposed to get cupcakes for the office party. There's a monthly birthday party for everyone and I was supposed to get the cupcakes."

"When is the party?"

"Today, at 3:00."

"Oh, you have plenty of time! How many do you need?"

"Uh, 20 or so." Sally's mind scrambled – she was

supposed to get the order in yesterday for pickup today.

"Hang on." Tessa said as Sally started to look up Screaming Mimi's Cupcakes on the Internet, "You get them from Mimi's?"

"How did…" She knew better to even finish the question as she had long ago stopped asking these *how did you know* questions of Tessa. "Yes."

"Okay I'm gonna order two dozen and they'll be ready at 2:30. Don't they give you guys administrative assistants?"

"No, well we have them, but this wasn't their job. It was mine." Sally admitted.

"Well it's done now, no worries. Go and have your lunch. I'll talk with you later. Have a good time at your party now." Tessa added.

"I will, and thank you Tessa." They each clicked off, leaving Sally wondering what had just happened. Lorna always said that Tessa worked in mysterious ways. And Sally was inclined to agree. But there was something intrusive about this, Sally felt. How can someone who is so helpful and generous and kind, be so exhausting?

Tessa had made her first million during the 1990's with the advent and widespread distribution of personal computers. With Quill, whose background was in medical and robotics engineering, Tessa had came up with several inventions that bridged the gap between "sighted people and the rest of the world," as she put it. It was the early days of computing then, and her inventions, both software and hardware, made computers accessible for the blind and "other" abled. Then Quill and Tessa went a step further by using the technology she invented for life style aids for the elderly. But Tessa mainly stuck with her original voice control devices for the blind and earned contracts from the government and several large-scale corporations, who used these micro- hardware devices in everything from GPS systems to security systems to animal training. Tessa --

a rock star in the world of geek. And the multi-multimillionaire who just ordered office cupcakes because Sally had dropped the ball.

Sally took a deep breath and asked herself why she was so irritated today. Then she remembered the cancer screening appointment with the gyno this morning. "Oh right, that was irritating," she said aloud. Did Tessa know about that? Is that why she called? Does she get irritated with Lorna, too, when Lorna started hounding everyone for their results? Then it dawned on Sally: it's the anniversary — of course! Tessa called to check on Sally. Tessa was getting a third party intelligence to gauge how Lorna was coping. Sally shook her head and grinned sheepishly to herself. Tessa is, she thought, a force to be reckoned.

Tessa walked the back path that led from her kitchen to her office in a converted barn, 32 steps. She wore a simple black dress and black flats. Her hair, an overgrown and curly unkempt nest of orange and auburn, bounced along animatedly.

"Hola, Senior Perez." She called out.

"Buenos días, Rojo." Senior Perez called back from flowers that lined either side of the path.

Tessa stopped and turned, facing Senior Perez. Senior Perez stopped his weeding and looked up at his boss. He looked at the path ahead of her, making sure it was clear to the door of the converted barn, and then back to her face for a moment.

"Rojo?"

"Yes?" She answered her head turned up as if listening for something.

Just then the side gate swung open and Quill walked through. He was wearing his best black suit and hiking shoes.

"Senior Quill is here." Perez finished.

"Yes, Perez. Will you put together a bouquet for me, some of the roses and some of the wild flowers? We're going to the graveyard."

"Yes, of course. Will I be driving? I am in my work clothes."

"No, Quill is driving."

Quill sauntered up the path, his tall lanky frame stooped with age.

"Senior Quill!" Perez's tone was scolding.

Quill whirled back around to face Perez and the gardener made a gesture toward his own crotch. Quill looked down and saw his shirttail sticking out of his pant's fly.

"Oh, gracious! Thank you, Perez." Quill tucked his shirt back in and zipped up his fly.

"Are you ready?" Quill asked Tessa as they finished the walk to the barn.

"Yes, I need to make a call first. And there is something I need to talk to you about. But it's a long story, so do you want it before we go to Lynn, or after?"

"Am I in trouble?" Quill asked.

"No. It has nothing to do with *you*. It's just some information that came to me … well, that I – it doesn't matter. It's information that I'm not sure what to do with." Tessa said softly before turning back to the door and typing in a four-digit code into the keypad. A click sounded and she said, "Tessa" loudly into the speaker.

Quill leaned around and said deliberately, "Clark Kent" into the speaker.

The door unlatched and they went inside.

"What's it about?" Quill asked anxiously, sitting down, "I won't be any good this afternoon. We should talk now."

"It's about Sally."

"Sally?" Quill was surprised. As far as he was concerned Sally was without reproach in every way.

Tessa sat down at her desk and pulled a file out from under her blotter. "You may want to sit down for this."

CHAPTER 3

SALLY

At 1:30 p.m., Sally got up from her desk and walked out her office. She was going to treat herself at the French Bistro on Market Street before going to the Screamin' Mimi's bakery and picking up the cupcake order. Despite the invasive morning, she had she was feeling relaxed. She stopped by the head administrative assistant's cubicle. "Katie, I'm going to lunch and then I'm going to swing by and pick up the cupcakes."

"Oh that's right -- it's today." Katie perked up instantly, her youthful exuberance bubbling up.

"Can I get you anything while I'm out?" Sally asked. Katie might be *just* a young administrative assistant to a lot of the higher-level managers, but Sally had seen Katie in action. And Sally knew Katie's secret: Katie was a highly efficient paper-pushing machine. Paper crossed Katie's desk only once before it was dispatched to the proper personnel. In the land of mind-numbing bureaucracy, under seizure-inducing fluorescent-lit clerical errors, Katie was a constant creeping magma of administrative accuracy. It was important to Sally that she kept Katie on her good side and treated her with respect. Katie might end up being her boss in a few years.

"Milk, please, two percent."

"I'm going to eat at the Bistro. They have the organic milk there, how's that sound?"

"Mmm." Katie smiled her approval.

Sally began walking out and over her shoulder tossed, "See you in a bit."

As Sally walked out of the federal office building she looked both ways before she jay walked across the street.

In February 1999, Sally Soucek's parent's car slipped off the icy Connecticut roadway into a ravine where they both died in the fiery blast. Sally took a week off work at the law offices of Bradley, Diamond and Baker in New York City to arrange their memorial, clean out their house, and hire estate sellers. She attended to her duties carefully and, as some commented, quite coolly.

In April that same year she received a postcard from New Zealand. It had three dolphins on the front. On the back Bill and Margaret Smythe wrote, "Today we swam with dolphins! Hope you are well!" Sally took the postcard with her into her small kitchen and turned on the hot water kettle just as Margaret Smythe, or whatever she was calling herself today, had taught her. She inspected the stamp and edges of the card before steaming it over the kettle and pulled back the picture of the flailing dolphins. "Thank you for taking care of the house and estate, Darling. We do hope all is well and perhaps you could take a vacation down under sometime. Love, Mom and Dad." Sally pursed her lips in disappointment and shook her head as she took a match and lit the postcard; dropping it into the sink she let it burn until she dowsed it with the boiling water.

Sally had spent most of her life being raised by her father's mother, Grandma Soucek, outside New Haven, Connecticut. When Sally was nine years old they had moved to Phoenix, Arizona only to have Sally return to a Connecticut boarding school at age 14. Her parents had been a foreign-service workers in embassies around the world. Between them, they spoke 11 languages, fluently. Postcards were a communications staple for her parents and they all read the same "Today we *fill in the blank*. Hope you are well." It wasn't until Sally's tenth birthday during a visit from her parents that she learned the steaming trick from Margaret or Barbara or Lucy or whatever she was calling herself then.

The summer between graduating college and entering law school, Sally was staying with Grandma Soucek in Phoenix. Sally knew that her Grandfather had died at the end of World War II. But that summer she learned that although not a household name, Grandpa Soucek had been somewhat of a World War II war hero. Grandma went through an old metal chest and showed Sally his medals and commendations signed by generals and both Presidents Roosevelt and Truman. It was Grandma's wish for her granddaughter to travel and get some public service under her belt before entering law school. She encouraged Sally to take a year off and do aide work in war-torn Bosnia. Despite Sally's reticence, on the subject phone calls were made, strings were pulled, and a year deferment to law school had been accepted. That August, Sally and many other fresh-faced aide workers boarded a plane to Bosnia for six months abroad.

With the ravaged remains of a horrifying war and genocide laid in front of them, the aide workers stayed close together in groups of 4 or 5. Sally's group did not have medical or engineering knowledge; they were couriers and did some food and medical transportation with their Cyrillic translator. Sally had been given a handgun with the completely plausible explanation that her looks posed a danger to her and others. She was half Chinese and half

Caucasian, but she looked like she could be from Hungary, Russia, or Bosnia. For Sally, the first month was all about adjusting her thinking, learning the ropes, and pushing through fear.

Somewhere in her second month it slowly became apparent that she and her group were being groomed. The weekly meetings that began as simple orientations, CISM's (Critical Incident Stress Management) training and operation goals had become more of debriefings about the areas they were transporting aide to, and who and what they had seen there. And with the Cyrillic translator, they were making more and more stops back and forth along the way to the aide distribution centers.

But the dawning moment came for Sally at the end of her third month abroad when she was asked to "make a drop." Make a drop. It was a phrase she had heard before, over dinner with her parents. Sally had never been told exactly what her parents did for a living. Once she was told they were janitors for the American Embassy in Japan. Then they were translators in the American Embassy in Turkey. By the time she was in college she had figured it out -- they worked for the CIA. She would have been happier knowing they were janitors.

Sally realized then what this time abroad really was, a recruiting trip. She had been teamed with someone from a different group, from the nursing staff, and they were to "make a drop" outside a village where they were taking medical supplies. Just the two of them this time, no translator. Sally felt sick to her stomach. She was working for the CIA, just like her parents, and Grandma Soucek had set her up for it. But this was against her will! She did not want to work for the CIA, she did not want to make this drop. But what would happen to her if she refused? Would this go on some kind of permanent record –that she had refused service during an aide mission? How could any parent do this to a child? She understood fully that this drop was some kind of initiation or graduating exercise. This was the first step that led into the murky underworld. And she had no choice in the matter. This was the real reason she had been given the gun.

During and after law school, Sally had been approached several times to join the clandestine operations with varying degrees of threats and promises. She was a shoe-in, a third generation legacy; she could name her port of call. Bullshit. She always turned them down flatly. So when she received that postcard in April 1999 she saw an opportunity. If her parents could make a break from their past, so could she. And where is the best place to hide? She changed her last name to Thompson and applied for a job at the Federal Housing Administration in New York City. The CIA had not approach her since.

A few years later, Sally met Lorna, and Sally fell instantly in love. Lorna's long blonde hair, lean athletic build, and the hint of a southern drawl mesmerized Sally. Lorna had been looking for a source, doing background investigations into a HUD scandal and had tricked Sally's administrative assistant into scheduling a meeting with her. The act of tricking Sally's assistant, who Sally had privately named The Viper, could not have been easy and that act alone made Lorna seem all the more interesting to Sally. So in order to keep seeing Lorna, Sally devised her own plan of giving only small bits of information out each time they met at various restaurants and coffee houses. But finally Lorna had enough of the Sally's game and said, "You seem really nice and I'd like to date you, but I have a deadline and would like to keep some semblance of journalistic integrity here."

But Sally would have to wait an entire year before being able to win over Lorna. That didn't happen until the fateful trip to Atlanta to meet Lorna's family where Sally witnessed the naked abandon with which Lorna's family shared their messy emotions with one another. Sally had never met a family like Lorna's and found she enjoyed their honest albeit messy emotions. She saw their unity and respect for one another.

Lorna's father had grabbed Sally around the shoulders and said in his deep southern drawl, "You know I was afraid she'd run you over like a Mac truck, but you held in there. That's good enough for me." This family was unlike anything Sally had ever experienced and she liked it. She wanted nothing more at that moment than to feel a part of them, and she knew she must never let them down. She must never let them know who her parents really were or what she had done.

Today was Thursday. The sun beat a blinding path through the windows at the Lunch Bag Diner. Annie sat at a long table with five of her co-workers with her hand cupped around her forehead to shade her eyes. Annie's deep auburn hair, cut into a bob, hung a couple of inches above her shoulders and was pulled back by a barrette while she ate. The online marketing group, CreSt, or Creative Strategies met with their "Out of Office Staff", the OoOS, every Thursday for lunch either in the city or in the East Bay. Annie was an OoOS and today they met on Ohlone Island, which was considered East Bay. The city dwellers from CreSt had all agreed they liked to meet on Ohlone because they got to ride a ferry. Two of the OoOS were missing. One was Kevin, whom Annie considered a not nice person, a turd in fact, and she didn't care why he was not there. Sharon was missing too. Annie knew where Sharon was but wasn't telling and hoped Sharon was going to be okay. These other people, the OoOS section of CreSt, despite their cooler-than-thou-nonchalance, were sharks. And Annie liked to think people like herself and Sharon as dolphins.

Heather St. James, wearing her oversized sunglasses, sat across from Annie out of reach of the powerful sunrays. Heather opened her mouth letting food dribble out and shook her fork around as she spoke, "Annie, I need to get the updated catalogue from you." She said it, Annie noticed, just in earshot of their boss.

"I sent it on Wednesday." Annie put her fork down and assumed a defensive posture.

Heather shook her head and continued eating and speaking at the same time. "No, I needed the *updated* one."

Annie looked down to the table where half-eaten chunks of food and bits of spittle launched from Heather's mouth were landing dangerously to her own plate. Annie leaned over to her laptop and spun it around, "This one. This catalogue? The one in my sent folder?" Annie spoke louder now.

Heather looked at the laptop. "That one didn't have the new price fonts on it." Heather nodded and smiled. "The client really needed it and I put him off for a day or two but I'm going to need it ASAP."

Jeremy, Annie's boss leaned around and piped in, "We shouldn't *put off* a client for any reason." He looked pointedly at Annie. "Let's get on that, okay?"

Annie nodded her head, "Of course."

Lorna rode her bike in the bike lane past the churches; several converted bungalows that were now dental practices and 12 storefront nail salons. She and Sally had bought a new car when they moved, but they had little use for it on the island as most of the main arteries had wide bike lanes. This is the sort of thing that sets the island apart from the other towns and cities in this country, Lorna thought, as she took a deep breathe of the perfumed salty air. I have never lived in a place that smells this good, nor where I took as many types of antihistamine. The scents of roses, honeysuckle, rosemary, and lavender wafted year round here. Lorna was feeling invigorated and the black mood that had followed her that morning was burning off like the morning fog.

Annie left the meeting at the Lunch Bag feeling deflated. She didn't understand Heather's animosity. Every Thursday someone would get some kind of shit from Heather. Always the same thing, Heather would call out the targeted person for some thing the targeted person hadn't done, or did wrong when Heather had made her instructions astoundingly clear. Delay of game, Annie decided to call it. Heather's delay of game, which is always just long enough to make Heather feel control by leaving out details to the rest of the staff or "losing" a file. She has the ear of the clients who have the ear of Jeremy and she always manages to make herself look like she's actually valuable to the creation of the marketing products. How could Jeremy not see this? Nah, Annie thought, Heather makes Jeremy think she is working hard, which she isn't, but as long as she seems to be taking responsibility that leaves Jeremy off the hook. There's got to be an easier way to make money, Annie thought.

Lorna hitched her bike onto the bike parking rack and fastened her helmet through the chain, locked it, and made her way across the parking lot to the museum's storefront. Because of the tinted windows she could not tell that it was closed for the day until she was right out front of the doors. "You're kidding me," she said aloud.

"Lorna!" Annie's soprano voice rang across the parking lot as she turned to see her friend and waved.

Lorna and Sally had made fast friends with Annie and her husband Tim. The close proximity of their homes and the fact that both Annie and Lorna worked from home gave them plenty time to chat and hang out. Tim was a human resources manager and like Sally was an avid photographer. He had privately come unglued when, after a month of knowing Lorna and Sally, he'd put together that the Tessa person Lorna kept referring to was *The Tessa*. After seeing a family photo of Lorna's he went home and dug out old copies of Entrepreneur and PC Daily magazines to show Annie. Both front covers were graced with Tessa's wild red hair. "Do you know who she is?" He demanded of Annie.

"Lorna says Tessa's her aunt-sister. Whatever that means,

I think it's a southern term." Annie answered. "I don't think it's a weird incest thing, Tim."

"No!" Tim showed Annie the magazines, "that Tessa!"

Annie looked at the cover and opened a magazine, "Oh," she laughed. "Yeah, Tessa Tollison. Lorna Tollison. I'll be damned." And tossed the magazine on the couch. As she left for the kitchen, Annie muttered under her breathe, "It doesn't explain why they rent then, I mean unless that a secret of the uber wealthy..." Tim just sat, stunned, staring at Tessa's picture.

As Lorna and Annie met half way in the parking lot, Lorna asked, "Hey, what's up?"

"We just had lunch at the diner, an office meeting, I guess. How are you?" Annie asked.

"Good, I was kinda playing hooky today and I wanted to look at the museum's new exhibit, but they're closed." Lorna answered. Getting a closer look at Annie's expression, Lorna furrowed her brow, "Was it a bad meeting?"

"No, just frustrating. I think there are just some people who are only able to feel good about themselves by damaging others."

"Yes. There are." Lorna agreed and acknowledged Annie's hurt.

"I hate them."

"We all do." Lorna smiled into Annie's green eyes. "But we'll get in trouble if we kill them."

Annie laughed. "That's true, I guess. But only if you get caught though."

"Next time drop a little ipecac in their food." Lorna looked down at Annie who stood about four inches shorter.

"Oh Lorna." Her eyes grew wide in horror, "That's horrible!" And smiled reflectively, "I really like it. Would you do that?"

"I've thought about it."

Annie jutted out her hip, mounting her hand on it and

countered, "But that's different than actually poisoning someone."

"It's not poisoning. Ipecac is medicine." Lorna argued.

Annie's eyebrow's raised up. "Oh, so you'd *medicine* someone?"

"Well, yes. If they needed some medicine, I *would* medicine someone."

Annie thought about it. "But that's not teaching someone a lesson to behave better --that's just making them sick."

"I know. I can't control people's bad behaviour, but it would make me feel better."

Annie lowered her voice. "That's kind of *crazy*, y'know?"

"I know! Which is why I haven't done it." Lorna nodded her head toward the museum, "What are we supposed to do wait for an old person to waddle by and ask them to open the museum?"

"The museum's hours depend on who can volunteer that day. So yes, *Crazy*, you are."

"Well that's not a good business plan. They're hanging by a thread as it is."

Annie agreed. "Neither is selling off your exhibits, but there you go. I'll play hooky for a little while, wanna get some coffee?" She suggested.

"Sure, why not." And with that the pair headed back to High Street past Ye Olde Ice Cream Shoppe to The Bottomless Cuppe which Lorna insisted on pronouncing both "P" sounds in Shop -pe and Cup-pe each time she went in.

"You're very curious about this island aren't you?" Annie asked as they walked.

Lorna drew out her answer, "Yes, I am."

"Why?"

"I don't know. It's a feeling I get, like it's lopsided." Lorna lowered half her body down and gimped up and down, walking in place.

"It's just a suburb that lost its identity when the military base closed and it's just sorta caught in limbo, I think." Annie explained.

"Yeah, I know all that and the early days when it was a playground for the rich and famous from San Francisco. But why are there 63 dental practices and 87 nail salons. *87*. How does a town of 43,000 people support that? For shits and giggles let's say of the 40,000 people half are women and let's be generous and say 10,000 of them get their nails done, that's like only like 110 clients per salon. And they'd have to get those nails done here, not in Berkley, not in Oakland, not in the city, every week for the salons to even survive. At the most they'd make maybe four to six thousand a month and that would have to cover rent, insurance, overhead. No, I just don't see it." It seemed to Annie that Lorna was ranting.

"You've really thought about this." Annie said as she opened the door.

They got their drinks and sat down, "So what exhibit were you going to see at the museum?" Annie asked.

"Oh they're suppose to have one on the original agriculture on the island and," she added conspiratorially, "they had an old chair in the *for sale* section, I keep thinking they'll drop the price on it."

"The one in the store front?" Annie flittered her fingers. "Ornate?"

"Yes, with the red?"

"Yeah, I liked it too, but I haven't seen it lately. I think it's a Chippendale."

"Really? Like an original?" Lorna was surprised.

"Yes."

"Damn, I bet they sold it! It was in great condition except a little knick on the armrest. I wanted to look at it again before Sally and I went to the antique festival this weekend."

"The one in San Jose?" Annie asked.

Lorna sipped her coffee and nodded.

"Tim and I are going too. We should car pool." Annie suggested.

Lorna put her coffee down and clapped her hands softly,

"Play date! Tim and Sally can take pictures and we can shop-pe!"

"I'm home!" Sally called out as if she had battled the King's brigades to make it there.

"I'm in the office!" Lorna called back.

Sally kicked off her shoes and slid around the hardwood floors to the office and said in a sing song-y tone "What's for din-ner?"

"What are you ma-king?" Lorna responded.

Sally threw her arms around Lorna. "Lorna on toast." And nuzzled her neck giving her a peck on the cheek.

Lorna drew back a little.

"What's wrong?" Sally asked.

"This is going to be a strange question. And I don't want you to get excited."

"Oh, okay," Sally set down on the window seat. "You're not pregnant or anything."

"No, that would be a strange miracle."

"But exciting."

"Did you come home today?" Lorna continued.

"No. Why?" Sally grew serious.

"Hmm. I'm not sure."

"What happened?"

"Okay, well, I left after I spoke with you. I went to the museum, which was closed, ran into Annie and we had coffee talk, then we rode our bikes home. I was gone maybe an hour or so. I came in and I finished this article –

"The Rebecca One?"

"No, this one's about pottery." Lorna answered.

"What do you know about pottery?"

"That's not the point." Lorna continued, "So I sit here for like two hours and I'm clacking away at the keyboard, I have my music playing softly and I hear the backdoor open. But I look in the kitchen and the back door is closed. What does that mean?"

"Patience learned how to open doors?"

"What? No!"

"We have a ghost?"

Lorna's eyes flashed hard at Sally. "No, Sally listen, I'm serious."

Sally realized this was true by Lorna's frown, "I'm sorry, what happened?"

"So I'm thinking what the hell, right? The door is closed and I did not hear it open. I also did not leave it unlocked when I left because I brought Patience and Fortitude inside before I left and locked it, like I always do."

"Okay." Sally was deadly serious now.

"I'm not hearing anything but I realize I haven't seen the boys since I got home. So I turn around and go to grab my keys off the key hook and they aren't there. Do I ever, *ever* not leave my keys on that hook?"

"No."

Lorna got up and walked out of the turret room and into the foyer, "I look down and my keys are here with the ring all jacked up. Look at it."

Sally picked up the key ring that had been cut and twisted apart.

"So then I just grabbed the whole set and leave. I run to the car and get in and go straight to the police station. Do you know what they told me?"

Sally felt her throat close up slightly, she wasn't sure she wanted to hear this. "No."

"I have a drafty home. I'm telling this asshole that I think someone has broken into our home and he tells me it's drafty. Do you believe that shit? I said 'Listen, I think there is an intruder in my home and I need police help. Are you refusing to aid me, the public? Isn't that in your oath?' And this little shit says, 'Ma'am, we're really short staffed today, all our guys are out on calls, if you'll just go home we'll send somebody by.' What the hell kind of bullshit is that?" A bead of sweat had banded across Lorna's upper lip.

"What did you do?"

"I came home and went through the house."

"You didn't get Annie or someone?"

"Annie wasn't home. I guess she left again."

"Why didn't you call me?"

"I did. Twice. I called your office twice. Once at the police station and after I got home again."

Sally jumped at her chance. "Okay, first of all stop calling my office. Call me on my cell. That way you'll always be able to reach me even if I'm away from my desk. Did the police come by?"

"No!"

"Okay, just take me through it again and show me this time."

Lorna went back into the office and walked Sally step by step through the incident.

Sally asked, "Did you talk to anyone on the phone in the time from when you got home to when you heard the door shut?"

"No." Lorna went into the kitchen, "And look at this." She shook the back door handle; "this was not loose like this when I left. I think it got jimmied or something."

"So," Sally concluded, "Someone broke in. Saw you were here – either before or after they cut through your key ring – and maybe something startled them and they left. Where are the boys?"

"Under the bed." Lorna lifted her eyebrows. This was not good news; the cats were friendly and known for their welcoming hospitality to visitors, giving ample time and chances for guests to pet them.

"Are they okay?"

"Yeah, they're just hanging out down there."

"So what time did this happen again?"

"About 3:00-ish."

Sally nodded, "I was at the office birthday party." She looked at Lorna's keys, "I'd think they've taken the house key, to come back. Where's that thing? That lucky charm thing?"

"I don't know, I must have dropped it on the way to the car or something -- maybe it's in the car, I don't know. It wasn't exactly the first thing I thought about."

"No, of course not. Do you want to go back to the police?"

"What the hell for? I'm just a hysterical woman who is scared of drafts."

"Okay." Sally hugged Lorna. "Okay, well I'm going to have some security put in here tomorrow and do you want to go to a hotel tonight?"

"No, I'm not getting scared out of my home. Fuck that."

"Okay."

"And leave our boys? They're scared shitless."

"Okay." Sally agreed nodding. "Me neither. Did you get the name of the person at the police department?"

"Evans."

"And I'll be writing a letter to the Chief of Police tomorrow as well as the city council, city attorney, county prosecutor and copy it to the newspaper, okay?"

"Wow, really?"

"Yes."

"That dude's gonna get fired."

"Probably not, but if we lodge a complaint it'll go in his record. What did you do after you got home again?"

"I went through the house, made sure the safe was still locked, made sure the boys were okay and looked through the closets and behind the shower curtain."

Sally decided that made perfect sense and nodded, "Good 'cause that's where the hatchet murderers hide."

"I know."

"Okay honey, I think we deserve a drink now. Don't you? It's not everyday that someone breaks in to murder your key ring." Sally went into the kitchen.

"Make mine a double please." Lorna followed Sally. "That's why I thought it was you. You've always hated that key ring."

Sally decided to break up Lorna's tension. "Only because it was blackmailing me."

Lorna played along. "For your secret diamonds?"

"Mmm," Sally nodded gulping her Chardonnay, "it is strange sweetheart, and you had a very unsettling day."

"Unnerving. That cop, Evans, was *not* about to help either." Lorna gulped the Chardonnay too.

"We'll take care of that and I'm going to have someone out here first thing tomorrow to put some extra security on these doors."

CHAPTER 4

ANTIQUE CARNIVAL

"Look at this! It goes on for miles." Tim said from the driver's seat, nodding his head forward at the stop and go traffic on 880 south. "We should have taken the train from Oakland."

Sally looked over at him. He had not shaved that morning, and bare patches of skin shone next to thick patches of stubble. His hair, thick and black and cut short, still had the pillow patterns in it.

Annie unlatched her seatbelt and pulled herself to the middle of the backseat of the Ford Escape. The highway was a parking lot, with cars inching ahead mercilessly. "Take the next exit – we'll go the up the back way, how we'd go from our old place."

"But that's a long way out of the way, and then we'd– " Tim argued.

Lorna unlatched her seat belt and scooted up next to Annie, "Tim, you're totally right. We should have taken the train, but this is getting painful. Let's take the exit."

"Sally?" Tim was looking for a teammate.

"Sorry, man. I'm lost as it is." Sally deferred.

"Back way it is, then." Tim carefully pulled into the emergency lane and drove the mile ahead to the next exit.

The San Jose Antiques festival only happens twice a year due to the vast scale of the event, which spans the entire downtown area. The set-up alone takes a couple of days, closing downtown streets and parks. Shoppers begin staking out parking in their cars and campers the night before the event. People arrive from all over the West Coast to sell, trade, barter, and buy each other's stuff. Museum dealers, Hollywood prop houses, collectors, and everyday people converge to stroll the street stalls, eat gourmet street food by local chefs, and enjoy the atmosphere which is part carnival and part shopping frenzy.

Realizing they would have to walk a mile just to get to the festival, the two couples poured out of the Escape still lamenting that they had not thought far enough in advance to take the train. It was a gorgeous day for the fair, warm and sunny with a slight breeze coming in off the ocean. Tim and Sally wandered ahead of Lorna and Annie, their cameras proudly strapped over their shoulders. Both peering ahead intensely, hunting for that first good shot. "I wish I had known about the break-in, I could have installed that security system for you guys."

"I just wanted it done as soon as possible." Sally answered.

"Right. I can see that."

"It doesn't bother me that we got broken into, cause that's just going to happen. It bothers me that it was so bold. Y'know, Lorna was there the whole time! What if she caught him, or her?"

"Then, I'd feel bad for the robber." Tim said.

"Please." Sally snorted, "The last time she got mugged in New York she tossed her wallet out and when the guy went to pick it up she kicked him in the ass so hard he fell into the street. She just picked her wallet back up and kept walking."

Tim started laughing. "No, she doesn't back down from a challenge very easily."

"I'm worried it'll get her shot one day." Sally continued, "Desperate people do desperate things. I know putting in a system after you get robbed is reactionary, and if the police would have been more helpful I don't think I would have done it, but they really just had this oh-well-that-happens attitude. So I just wanted to feel secure in our home again. How do you know about security systems?"

"Oh my dad was a cop – here in San Jose as a matter of fact. My brother and I used to install them for people as a summer job."

While looking at the vendors' antique kitchenware, Annie suddenly turned to Lorna and proclaimed, "I will never buy another brand new set of utensils again."

Lorna followed Annie's gaze, puzzled, but then realized that they had just passed multiple stalls spilling over with bins of mismatched silverware and laughed in agreement.

After several hours of picking through the treasures and trash, Lorna found a green bubble lamp circa the 1950's that she *had* to have and Annie bought several wooden ornate picture frames. Tim and Sally kept themselves busy with their cameras and Tim was drawn to anything that looked to be outdated electronics.

"You met Lorna's dad, Quill, when he came to visit didn't you?" Sally asked Tim.

"No, I was in San Diego that week." Tim answered.

"He's really into this stuff too." Sally said pointing to the electronic equipment.

"Yeah, Lorna said he was an engineer. I envy him, but it's just a hobby for me."

The food vendor area was strategically place in the center of the downtown area next to the park. The four decided it was time for some lunch and walked over to the grassy area where about 40 food vans had lined up, makeshift tables were scattered about and people were picnicking on the grass. Sally and Annie went together to a sandwich truck and stood in line while Lorna and Tim staked out a table where a family was picking up their wrapper remains and scooping up their bags for departure.

"After we eat, I'll go back and rent you guys a push cart to haul your stuff back to the car." Tim said as he settled himself into his seat and put Annie's frames safely near his feet. Lorna plopped the lamp into the chair next to her as a man approached the table.

"Is *someone* going to use this seat?" He demanded pointing at the lamp.

Lorna curled her upper lip at the man and with a slight up tick of her head said, "Yeah." It was the unmistakable New York *what are you going to do about it* edge she learned while covering a story about the plumbers' union in Brooklyn.

Tim smiled apologetically to the man, "Our wives – " but the man had already turned and left.

Lorna looked back at Tim and in an all-together pleased tone said, "That would be very nice Tim, thank you so much."

Tim worried his camera strap between his thumb and index finger for a beat, "Well, it will be easier for us."

"But here, let me get it," Lorna pulled out a ten dollar bill from her pocket.

Tim tried to stop her, "No, you guys paid for parking."

"Yeah, but you guys drove." Lorna insisted.

"No, you guys can get the coffee on the way home or something." Tim rejected the bill Lorna was shoving at him and pointed at the lamp, "I like the lamp though. It's retro fabulous."

"Thanks, it'll go in the living room I think."

Tim looked around conspiratorially, and put his hand in his windbreaker jacket and pulled it back out in a fist, "Look," he said displaying his palm, "what do you think of that?"

Lorna gasped. It was the ugliest ring she had ever seen. It looked like a vampire's chandelier with ornate black swirling metal and purple gems. It was like something a first grade boy would give to his young and pretty teacher. She leaned over his hand to hide her face. Why was it black? Was it made of lead? Lorna wanted to laugh, "Oh Tim, it's lovely, but isn't it a bit ornate for your hand?" She smiled the tension out of her face so Tim wouldn't catch on that she wanted to laugh.

"It's for Annie, an anniversary present." He seemed sincere.

"Oh! When is it?" Lorna asked.

"Valentine's Day." Tim blinked at Lorna's completely ridiculous question.

Lorna smiled, "Of course. Wow! That's thinking ahead." Why was this so funny to her? Think of dead puppies, think of dead puppies, she thought.

"Do you think she'll like it?" Tim placed it carefully in his jacket and patted the pocket.

"Yes." Lorna smiled and looked up at the sky stifling the laughter with a deep breath. She looked back down at Tim, who was still petting the outside of his jacket pocket.

"She likes purple."

Lorna's head tilted back up to the sky again, and she moaned a high-pitched stifled laugh and looked back down, with water brimming in her eyes. "Excuse me," she quickly pulled out a pocket tissue pack.

"Here," Tim scrambled and took the pocket pack from her as Lorna hid her head in her elbow crook and let off a shudder of laughter meant to be a sneeze.

"Oh, thanks," she took a tissue from Tim and wiped the water from her eyes. "It's the grass." She said as she turned to face Tim. "You don't have sisters do you?" She bit her lower lip.

"No," said Tim "just a brother in Hawaii. We don't really

talk much and I haven't seen him in a few years."

"Hawaii!" Lorna exclaimed, "If I had a brother in Hawaii, we'd be tight. Like every holiday I'd send him his favorite – something – or I'd just bring it to him."

"Not my brother or his wife. He's very secretive. God knows why. He's an accountant. Miserly with his time." Tim said reflectively.

"Well that blows. Older or younger?" Lorna asked.

"He's older." Tim said, with just an edge of bitterness, Lorna thought.

"Oh, I see." Lorna quickly changed the topic, "Are you shooting black and white?" She asked indicating his camera.

"Just a couple of rolls, yeah. But I brought my digital too." Tim answered and started again, "Hey I was going to ask you – " but stopped.

"Yes?" Lorna wondered.

"Your aunt."

"My aunt?" Lorna furrowed her brow. "Oh, Tessa." She didn't bother correcting him by pointing out that Tessa was technically her sister; the eight-year age difference often threw people off.

"I have an idea." Tim blurted out, "Do you think I could talk to her about it, when she visits next?"

"Do you want her phone number?" Lorna shrugged.

"No, I'd rather talk to her in person."

"Tim, she's blind. Talking *in person* really doesn't do a whole lot for her." Lorna explained.

"Oh yeah, well not like that…"

"It's not like you can *show* her an idea." Lorna continued.

Tim looked defeated.

Lorna saw this look and added, "But absolutely – we'll have dinner or cook out, and you two could talk afterward. That way there won't be any pressure or awkwardness."

Tim looked panicked, Lorna thought. So she continued, leaning in a bit. "But if you really want to get her ear you should tell me your idea and I can get her softened up for you."

Tim shook his head, "No, I shouldn't have asked. That was wrong. I'm sorry Lorna." Tim let out a frustrated grunt and sighed, "I think my company's being bought out by Spectorgies."

Lorna thought for a moment, "Spectorgies? I thought they did defense contractor stuff, like bomb building."

"No .... well yeah, but they do a lot more than that now." Tim explained.

"So, are you going to talk about an invention you have, an idea you want to develop or like for a job in her company?" Lorna boldly asked.

"Okay, well one, an idea for an invention I have. I think I need a patent." Tim looked away toward the food trucks. "But if she had a position in human resources, I wouldn't turn it down. Why is she even in Atlanta? She should be here, near the technology." Lorna smiled, "Well, you can tell her that when she comes."

As Sally and Annie wound around other tables and picnickers on their way back, Tim smiled, "Thanks again."

"No problem. I hope works out." And with that, Lorna divorced herself from the result of Tim's request. Lorna often thought that there was a crazy gene that gets activated around fame and money and that the only way for a friendship to survive when that gene gets activated was to heed the request and quickly step out of the picture. But this was different. Tim looked really worried, almost desperate, Lorna thought.

"Hope what works out?" Sally asked.

"Tim has a massive brain tumor and I offered to have Tessa dig it out for him." Lorna spoke to Sally in a code she hoped Sally understood. Sally locked understanding eyes with Lorna. But Annie, standing in earshot, also understood Lorna's meaning, and she looked disapprovingly at Tim, who was looking hungrily at his sandwich.

"Well, that makes sense." Sally answered with equal,

measured sarcasm and put a sandwich down in front of Lorna, "Ham and Gouda, no tomato."

"We were talking about photography." Tim smiled.

"Here," Lorna pulled out four small packages of wet-naps from her purse, "BEFORE you eat with your hands, *Sally*."

Sally put her sandwich down obediently and grabbed a wet-nap.

Tim looked at Lorna's purse. "What else you got in there?"

"Lorna was a girly scout. She's always prepared."

"Who was your troop leader -- Rambo?"

Lorna smiled. "Yes, and she also taught us dirty limericks – wanna hear one?"

"No!" Said Sally, "Eat your sandwich."

Lorna took a bite, still smiling.

"You can tell me one after lunch." Annie whispered, digging into her sandwich.

Before they went back to the double rows of stalls, they stopped by the port-a-potties.

"Where's Tim going?" Annie asked, looking after Tim, who had crossed back over the food court area.

"He went to get a push cart for us." Lorna answered as they moved over to the portable sinks.

"Honestly, I have never seen such well maintained port-a-potties! And look at this port-a-sinky." Lorna claimed.

"And look," Sally joined in, "port-a-soapy," as she squirted a dollop of soap in her waiting palm and pumped the foot peddle for water.

"You're right," Annie agreed, "I've seen restaurants that could take a lesson from these port-a-people."

Lorna burst out laughing and gasped, "That's brilliant! The only way you can exit a bathroom stall is if you wash your hands first." She waved her hand up, "Wave of the future – how's that for clean technology?"

"Here." Sally began to take the lamp from Lorna's arms,

"There's an open bench. Annie, give me your frames and I'll have a seat and wait for Tim." Lorna looked back at the park benches longingly and Annie gratefully handed over her frames to Sally.

Annie and Lorna continued their perusing in front of a stall filled with ancient looking musical instruments. "Lorna, what were you and Tim really talking about when Sally and I came up with the sandwiches?" Annie asked straightforwardly.

"I can't tell you," Lorna answered before adding, "but I will give you a hint. Valentine's Day."

"Ooh, okay." Annie looked relieved.

"Let me ask you, is Tim color blind?"

"Practically. Something to do with his cones."

Lorna nodded knowingly, "Hmmm." That explained why he thought purple was Annie's favorite color when Lorna has never seen her wear that color.

"Why?"

"Nope. I gave you a hint and that was your clue."

"Come on," Annie cajoled her. "Tim's color blind – that's my clue?" Then it dawned on her. "Our anniversary … oh no! Tell me it's not another awful brooch."

"No. It is not." Lorna said confidently.

Annie sighed deeply.

"I was worried," Annie admitted.

"About what?"

"I was worried he was bugging you about Tessa. You know she's like the nerd Rock Star, right?"

"Whatever. She snores like one." Lorna did not want to betray Tim's confidence, but then thought better of it. She would not want to be caught keeping a secret or even seeming to be and lose Annie's trust over something so silly. "Look, I don't want to get caught in the middle of anything with you two. He did ask me and I said yes. I think he's just worried about his job and if taking a meeting with Tessa, one he can brag about and look important or whatever, helps him, then all the better." The two women stopped perusing the stalls and faced one another before Lorna continued, "Annie, she's my family. She built a brand, like a candy bar, but it's not her. She's not a candy bar, y'know? And you guys are our friends, so if using Tessa's stature, or whatever, helps Tim – then good."

"You're not annoyed by it?" Annie asked.

"Oh hell, yeah! Totally annoyed with him. I've been seen as a stepping-stone to Tessa for years now. I hate it, like I'm sure kids of ministers and wives of, like, senators or any public figures are annoyed with it. But that's the territory, you learn to surf it."

"Oh. But you know, even if you weren't related to Tessa, he'd still like you guys."

Lorna wanted to move on, "Sure, but what I didn't know was that Spectorgies did other things besides defense contracting. Maybe he and Tessa can share information." Lorna shrugged, "Who knows."

Annie still looked worried.

"Annie, it sounds to me like nothing has happened yet. Tim is worried that with a takeover, Spectorgies is going to dump him and he's just being proactive. If I were you I'd rather see him asking around and getting his ducks lined up for a worst case scenario then doing nothing and hoping for the best." Lorna turned her attention back to the stalls and Annie followed.

"That's true – he does like to work ahead."

Lorna tilted her head and focused on a wooden table on display, "Tim's a smart guy. I wouldn't worry too much," before moving on to the next stall with Annie in tow.

"He *is* very smart." Annie said, only half paying attention to the stalls they ambled past. "I just worry, because, well, it's Spectorgies. I mean what do they want with a human resources outfit? They build bombs and planes. They run private security firms in foreign countries."

Lorna stopped abruptly and quickly did an about face on Annie – so abrupt that Annie turned too. Looking around, Annie spotted Tim and Sally who were paused at a stall filled with old electronics and phonographs. Annie looked back at Lorna who looked like a Pointer focusing on the water fowl, "What is it Lassie?" She said to Lorna. "Do you sense Timmy? He's rescued Sally with a shopping cart."

Lorna either ignored her or didn't hear her, but mumbled out of the corner of her mouth, "Annie, look over my shoulder, is that or isn't that the chair from the museum?"

Annie craned her head around Lorna's back and looked at the chair before moving around and touching the notch on the armrest, "That's odd."

Tim and Sally caught up with them. One look at Lorna and Sally said, "Uh oh, what happened?"

Lorna turned to Sally and pointed to the chair, "What do you think of that?" Lorna demanded.

Sally took a few steps toward Annie and the chair, and stepped back to Lorna, "It's 18 hundred dollars for an old chair." She said flatly.

"We saw one just like it at the Ohlone museum. See! It's missing a notch in the arm rest." Annie said.

"So?" Tim joined in, "It's probably the same chair."

"Maybe it's from a set." Sally said.

Lorna screwed her face up at Sally, "You think they hand carved these Chippendale chairs and then cut a gouge out of the arm rest so they all would match?"

"Sure," Sally shrugged, "People are weird. They were weird in the 1800's and still are today."

Annie looked puzzled, "Can they do that? Sell a chair from a museum?"

But Tim added, "No, it's community property. But I thought you said they sold things out of the museum, too."

"Yeah," Sally agreed with Tim, "maybe it's a co-op thing where they put antiques on consignment and like put a museum around the antiques to add nostalgia."

"Hang on," Lorna stepped through to the back of the display where the purveyor sat in a lawn chair, his head dangling down on his chest. "Excuse me!" Lorna poked him in the shoulder. The purveyor's head snapped up and his hand flew up to his shoulder where Lorna poked him, his bloodshot eyes strained to focus on her. "I just love that chair out front, is it from an estate sale? Are there others?" The purveyor adjusted his ball cap and long stringy grey and put his large square glasses on.

He rocked back and forth to gain momentum to get to his feet. Once there he yanked up his pants, rubbed his grey scruffy beard, looked to the chair, and cleared his throat before he answered. "I'll have to check my receipts." He wiped the corners of his mouth and scratched his perfectly firm beer gut, "I don't have them with me today."

"Do you have a shop? Somewhere to stop in at?" Lorna continued.

"You're in it. But if you're interested in that chair, we can arrange something." He offered.

"Okay," Lorna eyed him suspiciously. "Let me confer with my friends." She wound her way around the side tables and chairs back through to the front of the display where the rest of her group stood watching. "Well, he's not sharing *anything*." She hissed to their faces that were looking past her now. Sally's face was oddly screwed up and her eyes were fixed to the distance.

"It's not – " The purveyor's gruff voice startled Lorna. She lurched forward bumping into Sally and turned around. The purveyor reached a hand out to steady her, "Sorry, it's not a replica. I'm sure about that, I've been doing this for thirty years."

Lorna said flatly, "Right, you're an expert. If you can give us a minute privately *please*." Lorna stretched out her arms and gently moved her friends forward. Annie sensed Lorna needed to talk to Sally alone and pulled Tim off to the side as well.

Sally squared off to face Lorna directly, "Honey, you're not serious about spending that kind of money are you?"

Lorna's brow furrowed, "But is it illegal?"

"For a chair?" Sally stole a glance at the chair, "Maybe."

"No, what Annie said – is it illegal to buy it if he can't prove ownership or where he got it?" She asked.

"Not if you buy it in good faith. What do you mean?"

"That's the chair from the museum, I'm sure of it." Lorna said.

Sally struggled to find Lorna's logic, "So?"

"So, if he stole it, it can be returned. That poor museum doesn't have the same access to money and power as the Museum of Fine Arts."

Sally paused, her eyebrows lifted, "Well, maybe they sold it to make ends meet."

Lorna put her hand to her hip, "That can't be legal, Sally. Someone donates antiques, takes the write-off, and then the recipient sells it for a profit?"

Sally shook her head, "Two words. Salvation Army. But," Sally continued, "you had said they've had floods and fires. If they took an insurance write-off for destroyed property, then it might be fraud." She took Lorna's hand into hers, "And that is something, my sweet muffin, a federal attorney's partner doesn't get involved in."

Lorna rolled her eyes at Sally as Annie approached, "So what did you decide?" Annie asked.

"That Sally hates museums." Lorna announced.

"Is that a deal breaker?" Annie smiled, while thinking that this could be a really long ride home.

Sally explained, "Lorna thinks there is something hinky going on."

Annie felt relief, "Of course there is. Look around you." And indicated the people milling about with their valuables.

"With the chair and the museum." Sally felt a lost battle coming on as Tim now approached with the cart.

"Sally, I found a stall in the last aisle with more old

electronics, I think there's an old sonar. Want to join me?" Gratefully, Sally followed Tim away from the stall.

But Annie caught the edge of the shopping cart as it rolled past and chose her place on the domestic battlefield, "Leave the cart with us." Tim lifted his arms, surrendering the shopping cart and moved on with Sally before Annie turned to Lorna, "Now, what is this about?"

"Annie, you know that's the chair from the museum, right?" Annie stole a last glance of the chair and nodded before Lorna continued, "So, what's it doing here?"

"Okay, maybe they sold it to this guy. Or … or maybe he dumpster dove it out and fixed it back up."

"After a fire?" Lorna sneered at the chair.

Annie nodded and kicked some dirt below her foot, "So this is incongruent for you. And you're having a visceral reaction to the lack of a logical sequence."

"No … What? No, I want to know how this guy, Mr. Shleppy here, ends up selling a chair for 18 hundred dollars when it was being sold for 21 hundred at the museum and he can't or won't tell me he got it from. None of these other items are from the museum, I don't think. And those people at the museum weren't the negotiating sort, trust me, I tried…"

So this is why Sally gave up the battle, Annie thought, and gazed around her as Lorna continued, "or what if he stole it? How would you steal a chair?"

"Okay," Annie took the reigns of Lorna's runaway reaction, "here's what you do. See if he'll take a check. If so, then pay him and take the chair back to the island. Check in with the museum and find out whether or not something hinky happened. Either way you'll be covered."

"They don't take checks here." Lorna scoffed.

"He might. You have to ask. He can't expect people to carry that kind of cash around." Annie said.

Lorna thought she liked this logic, "Right."

"And you'll have a couple of days to cancel the check - if

it was stolen." Annie continued.

"That is such a good plan. We can get their chair back, or I can have a cool chair. Thank you, I'm so glad you're here." Lorna turned on her heel to negotiate with the purveyor.

CHAPTER 5

IT'S IN THE GARAGE

Sally snickered to herself as she walked to the bus top on Monday morning. She loved how simple her life had become here. No more unexplained postcards that she'd have to burn immediately, no more offers she couldn't refuse from the Services. And the cherry on top was that her partner was completely outraged over a possible fraud at a local museum. Fraud nonetheless, but it *was* a chair. Sally had begun to really loosen up for the first time in her adult life, to breathe easier – no more looking over her shoulder. She loved the routine. Everything was quaint and predictable. Even Lorna's outbursts of indignity at injustices, real or imagined, made just enough waves to keep it interesting. There was an occasional earth tumbler, but no hurricanes or tornadoes, no terrorist attacks – which reminded her that she and Lorna needed to get together an emergency pack in case there was a major earthquake or even just an inconvenient one. That would be a great project for Lorna, perhaps get her mind off that stupid chair.

The low growl of the impending O Line bus caught her attention. As Sally made her way on board, she smiled at the elderly lady who sat in the same seat daily — the first seat on the right hand side of the bus – reserved for the elderly and handicapped.

"Jo sun." Sally nodded, greeting the elderly lady in the lady's native tongue.

"Jo sun." The woman smiled back at Sally as she did every morning, Monday through Friday, at 7:45 am.

Sally balanced herself deftly without hanging onto the straps dangling above her head. She pulled out her mp3 player and placed the ear buds in her ears. A new French Jazz piece she had downloaded sprung to life in her ears. As she adjusted the volume she felt several elbow nudges her back. She moved forward out of elbow nudging range and put the mp3 player in her pocket. The elbowing continued a moment later, and she turned around to see a New York Times newspaper in her face. She was stunned to see a yellow highlighted 'Friday December 15, 1995'. That was the month of the Dayton Peace Accords in Bosnia. Sally's blood ran cold. The paper was flipped around and a new date was highlighted, 'Monday February 8, 1999'. Her heart rose up to her throat. She did not see the headline; it was the day of her parents' alleged death. She felt white-hot, as sweat broke out across her brow. They had found her, and they wanted to talk.

Sally steadied her breathing and slowly, carefully moved her hand up over the newspaper and brought the paper down so that she and a young man were eye to eye. She held his gaze, steady and firm, till his eyes darted around before she caught them again and said simply, "No." She slowly turned her back to him.

As the bus rolled to a stop, the young man made a dash for the opened door in back and disappeared from Sally's sight. The elderly lady in the first seat had watched the whole episode and she now smiled and nodded at Sally in approval.

Sally nodded back without smiling and moved her gaze out the window. Her mind spun out of control. So this is where her life falls apart? Are there others on this bus? She scanned the passengers. Most faces she recognized. Had she noticed him before? How long had he been riding the bus with those stupid newspapers? These things don't just happen, they're planned, teams are in place, and there is always a goal. He was just a courier and she was his target. And he achieved his goal; he was probably making the triumphant call to his handler right now. Can these idiots not just pick up a phone and call her? Maybe her parents were really dead now and that was the message. Gradually, the shock began to wear off, and she began to go through the last two weeks in her mind. Had anything happened out of the ordinary? Had anyone mentioned anything odd? Lorna, Tessa, Quill … No! she thought. Fuckin' Hell. *Tim.* Tim was the only difference. But what could a human resources manager … her thoughts stopped. If Tim goes to work for Spectorgies, in human resources, then he's a perfect target for the CIA. Corporate Espionage. But that's not CIA territory, that's FBI or Secret Service. Maybe whoever is trying to contact her is just looking to vet Tim …

Sally had no memory of how she came to be sitting in her office, staring straight ahead.

Snap. Snap. Fingers waved in front of her face. Sally squinted up at a co-worker; the bubbly young woman greeted her, "Happy Monday. Lost weekend?"

The edges of Sally's mouth moved outward before she spoke, "No, I forgot my lunch."

"Tragic." The woman flung a stack of folders onto her desk. "Here are the files you requested. Sorry it took so long. If you forgot your wallet, too, I can float you till Friday."

"No, I've got it, but thank you. I just hate to trek out at lunch today, I've got so much to cover this week." Sally moved the files to the side of her desk. The woman was still talking as she walked out, but her words fell on Sally's deaf ears. Sally wished she could talk about this with Lorna. Lorna would know what to do. She must have been a strategist in another life. Sally knew she would have to come clean to Lorna, no matter what. This was just too close to home. "Okay."

The voice in her head sounded remarkably like Lorna's voice. "Here's what we'll do – nothing. The courier made his drop and you actually gave him an answer. That, if history tells us anything, should be the end of that. But if you reach out and inform Lorna of your past, then you'll need to pose it to her like this. Say: 'I have a problem that I need my best friend's help with.'" Sally stopped and redid this opening to Lorna several times before she realized she would simply have to turn power over to Lorna and admit to her lies. I'll have to move out for a while, Sally thought, and regain her trust. But I don't want to move out. I did it to protect her. No, I did it because I was ashamed and scared. She swirled around a paperclip on the desk with her fore finger. That will be plan B, telling Lorna the truth. Plan A is to do nothing. If I make no action, there can be no reaction. She took a deep breath and looked up at the fluorescent lighting suppressing a sudden urge to call Lorna. She determined not to do anything out of the ordinary; the call would have to wait until their normal lunchtime conversation.

Was there something strained in Sally's voice? Lorna asked herself as she hung up the phone and frowned at the stack of work on her desk, "Did that pile grow over the weekend?" In response, Patience rolled over and showed her his belly. She gave his belly a scratch before patting the stack of work on her desk, "All in good time, my pretties." Lorna walked around the house checking the sensors on the security system and opened the small metal box that sat on the shoe chest next to the front door. Sally had gone overboard, spent too much money and too much time building a false sense of security here. While researching an article about personal safety, Lorna had read a theory by a former robber- cum-security- expert who'd said if someone is bound to rob from you they will find a way, whether you have bars on your windows, locks on your doors, or alarms on your car. And although she wasn't inclined to then leave her doors unlocked for wayward thieves of opportunity, she did agree with him in principle. She walked out the front door and started to pull the door closed. Suddenly remembering her keys on the latch hook, she made a dive for the closing door. She snatched the keys up and shoved them in her pocket as she closed the door again. Picking up the newspaper from the front lawn, she headed to the O Line Bus stop at the end of the block. She opened the newspaper as she waited. The headline read: "Spectorgies In, Free Will Out." Lorna thought about this for a moment. I don't know who's more militant, the liberals or the military complex. She scowled. How could they be surprised? This *is* a military town. She read on through the details of how Spectorgies has been branching out into various areas including winning government contracts for the upcoming census and data processing projects. She folded the paper down as the bus approached, still thinking about the article. What Janusian thinking this island has – on the one hand Spectorgies means more island jobs and taxes, and on the other, it is seen as "public enemy number one" because it makes money on military actions in Iraq and Afghanistan. Or maybe, she thought, the people just like biting the hands that feed them. She thought about Colby Systems, another defense contractor, which also had offices on the island but you didn't see them getting picketed. The dichotomy fascinated Lorna.

The bell attached to the museum door hung precariously above the door jamb and twinkled when Lorna opened the door. An elderly balding woman, with a pronounced teased-up forward comb sweep, smiled as she entered. "Hello," said the forward sweep as Lorna struggled to look only at the woman's eyes, "have you been to our museum before?"

"Hi," Lorna locked eyes with the woman, "I have actually, I'm curious about some of the pieces from the exhibits."

"You'll have to talk to Mr. Holder."

Lorna expected more of an answer and was caught off guard. It was her turn to talk again and she smiled at the Sweep, "Is he here today?"

The elderly woman pressed her lips in a frown at Lorna, "Well, yes, but you'll just have to wait because I can't leave the front desk."

Lorna smiled at the woman again and moved over to the spinning bookrack. She took her time looking through the yellowed volumes of romances and mystery books. There was a 1956 cookbook that called for putting on your asbestos gloves before removing a chicken from the oven. Several moments later she heard whispering voices before turning back around to face the reception desk.

"I'm Mr. Holder, Ms. Wagginpuff said you wanted to speak to me." The uncommonly tall and lean elderly man wearing purple parachute pants and a Hawaiian shirt placed his interlaced hands in front of his abdomen.

I'm in a cartoon, Lorna thought, but matched his formal business tone, "Yes, I'm Lorna Tollison. I'm curious about the provenance of the antique furniture pieces. Are they donated to the museum?" *Provenance?* Where'd that come from? Stay in the moment; listen to his words.

Holder took a step closer to Lorna, forcing her to crane her neck up at an awkward angle. "Well most, we were able to purchase a few, before we fell on hard times. I always kept clear records of the provenance where I could, of course." His eyes lowered to the floor.

Lorna nodded giving a respectful beat of silence for his

loss, "There was a chair that sat in the front window. It was an antique mahogany Chippendale, a beautiful piece."

Mr. Holder nodded. "Yes, it was. It was left to us in a will. Are you interested in donating to us?"

"What happened to the chair?"

"It was ruined in the flood apparently." He said in a studiedly casual tone.

"Apparently. Like *obviously* it was? Or apparently, but you're not sure."

His smiled tensed as he bared his teeth to her, "Obviously. What *is* the nature of your visit today, Miss?" He asked in a faux patient tone.

"I'm curious about the chair."

He shook his head, lowering it again, "It's not here. What does it matter? We're in a deeply distressing time. What we need are donations and community outreach."

Lorna decided to go along with his train of thought, "I see. How good of you to recognize that. Community outreach is really what museums are about, aren't they?"

"We do enjoy playing our part, such as it is." He ho-hummed as he glanced at the clock behind Lorna.

"I know they pulled your funding, but that's temporary. They won't let the Island's Museum fall too far."

"It's really up to the community now." He drew out, "If we don't get some kind of backing we may end up packing it in, I'm afraid."

Hint, hint, thought Lorna.

"It's a simple matter of marketing, I should think. People are your greatest resource –

and well, the donations, I'm sure." Lorna laid it on thick.

Holder took a deep breath. "Yes. You're not interested in volunteering – perhaps wrangling some of those donations are you? A pretty woman like yourself, it would be a snap."

His obsequious whine was setting Lorna's teeth on edge. She hated his pants. And his shifty eyes. "Well, maybe," she said casually and looked around with just a smudge of disdain in her eyes.

"Well then," Mr. Holder began with a new bounce in his voice, "you'll want to speak with Mr. Hazinsky. He's our docent in charge of acquisitions."

He turned to leave, but Lorna continued, "I see. Well, what if I – " she paused and looked back at the store front and began again, "you see, I was at an antiques fair this weekend and I bought that chair. The one you just said was ruined in a flood."

Mr. Holder smiled patiently down at her, "that piece was quiet common," he said in educating tones, "but I hope you enjoy it and when you're finished perhaps you'll donate it back. If you'll excuse me." He turned and walked past the reception desk.

Lorna turned and left the museum, the twinkling doorbell drowning out her "donate my ass" as she left. She walked across the street to the Mexican restaurant muttering angrily. She ordered two tacos and an iced tea before she sat down at a table facing the museum's front door and stared ahead. After she ate her first taco she nodded to herself as she watched the sign on the front door being turned from "open" to "closed."

"Interesting," she said aloud.

As Sally finished off her lunch, she decided to take half a day off. She had been only able to compose herself for a few minutes at a time and was getting nothing done. When she called home, however, Lorna was on her way to the museum and seemed quite disinterested to hear that Sally would be home early. Sally hung up the phone with a sick feeling in her stomach. She left her office and walked down the street. She began feeling feverish when she entered the public law library on 7th and Mission, intent on an anonymous online search for dockets and orders containing the name Spectorgies or its aliases. The sheer volume of docket numbers that came up made her cringe. She quickly closed the open computer windows and rested her head in her hands. Her mind and heart were racing again. She took a deep breath and exhaled slowly. Gathering her bag up and slinging it over her arm, she looked around the small library assessing the situation. She needed to a place to go get her head straight before going home.

Sally left the law library and followed a winding path toward Chinatown, stopping several times to tie her shoes and glance in the store windows behind her. She ducked into a coffee house and promptly walked another direction to the borders of Chinatown where she found an open Buddhist Temple. As she entered, one of the monks greeted her with a deep bow, Sally returned the bow and, unquestioning, he showed her to a pad on the floor facing a giant smiling Buddha. She inhaled incense as she coiled herself onto the pad. She sat quietly as the thoughts left her mind, leaving only the relief of solitude.

She heard the soft shuffling of feet and began to slowly open her eyes, letting them adjust to the big fat smiling Buddha in front of her. She smiled back and checked her watch. It was 3:00. She felt relaxed and refreshed, but good heavens, she had been sitting there for two hours. Her knee cracked as she stood up and bowed to the Buddha. She bowed more deeply to the monk at the door and dropped a five-dollar bill in his golden plate as he opened the door for her. Sally walked through the door, letting the California sunshine wash over her. She was ready.

After a second hour of staring at the museum's front door and not seeing anyone come or go, Lorna picked up the various napkins, drink bottles and salad bowls from the table and left. Where could she get more information? Ah, the library of course. She headed out to the new library across town. She thought as she walked along the storefronts of High Street that the museum had been a complete bust. Or was it? Now at least she knew that Holder was hiding something. Why else would he keep changing the subject? And that poor old volunteer chained to her desk like that. No wonder they couldn't keep volunteers! Lorna rounded the corner and saw the new library, which had opened in August. It was a two-story state of the art cement monstrosity, completely out of place amidst the celebrated Victorian architecture of the island. But it had central air and heating, not something the rest of the island's older buildings and homes enjoyed, and it had all the amenities: a café, meeting rooms, free Internet, and self-checkout.

Lorna walked in and straight up to the second floor research area. She pulled out a couple of local history books from the shelves and settled in.

Sally walked in the front door. The smell of ammonia-tainted cat urine smacked her square in the face. She closed her eyes to combat the offensive odor then she tripped over the chair that had been placed in the middle of the foyer. Fortitude greeted her with a meow. Patience came out of the bedroom stretching.

"Of course," she said to them, "it's an 18 hundred dollar toilet to you guys! What were we thinking? Lorna!" Hearing nothing back, she called out again as she checked the bedroom and bathroom. It dawned on her that Tim and Annie were coming over for a bar-b-que that night, so Lorna must be at the grocery market. Sally grabbed the chair and carried it out to the garage. She set it off to the side and arranged a blue tarp over it. When she came back in the back door, the phone was ringing.

"Hello?" Sally answered the phone in the kitchen.

"Oh hi – this is Annie."

"It's Sally."

"Thanks. You two are sounding more and more alike on the phone."

"So I hear. Lorna's dad said the same thing."

"Is there anything we can bring over tonight?"

"You should call Lorna's cell. I think she's at the grocery now."

"What are you doing home so early?" Annie asked.

"I took half a day." Sally explained.

"Good for you. I'll call Lorna. Bye."

"See you later." Sally hung up just as Lorna blasted through the front door.

"That was so bizarre!" Lorna exclaimed.

Sally craned her head around the kitchen door, "What …"

"AAAHHH!!!" Lorna's body convulsed as she threw her purse at Sally. "What the fuck!"

"I'm sorry, I'm sorry! I didn't mean to scare you." Sally raced over to Lorna and threw her arms around her. "Sshh."

"Holy shit. You scared the *hell* out of me." Lorna grabbed her chest.

"I'm sorry. … What was so bizarre? Who were you talking to? 'Cause I thought you were talking to me." Sally quickly explained.

"No, I was just thinking out loud. That museum – the people who work there are so bizarre. What are you doing home?" Lorna asked.

"I called you, remember? Did you get the groceries?"

"Oh right. For what? Oh shit, the bar-b-que. Shit, no. Wait, where's the chair?"

Sally paused for a beat. This was not going to be good. Lorna was clearly excited about something and she just had a scare. Sally braced herself, "The boys peed on it."

Lorna's mouth dropped open, "Oh no, they did not. Where is it?"

"It's in the garage."

Lorna's right eyebrow lifted, "You put – my Chippendale chair – out, " she paused for effect, "in the *garage*?"

Sally chose her words carefully this time, "It smelled like

ammonia cat pee. Can't you still smell it?"

Lorna flared her nostrils. "You didn't try to blot it down?"

"Lorna, I just got home. I smelled it, tripped on it and took it to the garage, where I carefully placed it to the side and put a tarp over it. I got in and Annie called, then you came bursting in like a hurricane."

Lorna slowly eyed Sally from toe to the tip of her head. Sally recognized this. It was the brain coil and Lorna was about to strike. The tirade that came out of Lorna's mouth next made no sense. It was an eruption of curses and demonic slang in several languages and without regard to race, religion, gender, or sexual identity. These tirades happened, occasionally, when Lorna felt threatened or persecuted – whether real or imagined. They just goes on and on, never repeating, and she never took a breath. Sally watched Lorna's face go red. Lorna must be able to do the circular breathing Sally had heard musicians talk about.

Finally Sally said, "I'm going to the market."

As the door closed she heard Lorna scream, "Yes! You should!"

CHAPTER 6

DINNER AND A PLAN

Had Lorna not been side-tracked all day, she would have marinated the ribs all morning in dry rub spices and slow smoked the them over hickory chips on the grill in the afternoon (which is exactly what her guests expect when she barbeques). Unfortunately for her guests this was not to be. So Sally took it upon herself to recreate the menu at the grocery, picking up hamburger, meatless hotdogs, and assorted side salads at the deli counter. Annie would bring the drinks and pie for desert, so all and all, not half bad for a last minute scramble to save dinner. When Sally got home, Lorna was in the garage, staring down at the cat urine soaked chair. Sally parked the car and got out, "Mission accomplished," she said as she opened the trunk and pulled out the grocery bags and stopped to give Lorna a forlorn smile.

Lorna snapped out of the melancholy and accepted Sally's smile by returning a smile, "Excellent, the grill is warming up."

"It sounds like Holder just didn't want to deal with it,"

Tim said between bites.

"And anyway, you can't prove anything, really, not fraud at least." Sally said before taking her next bite.

Lorna stared at the plop of potato salad on her plate. After 4 tacos and 2 taco salads this afternoon, she was simply not hungry. Annie put her meatless hotdog down. "Lorna, I'm so sorry, I had no idea this would cause you so much grief."

Lorna looked up from her plate and over to the empty chair that sat next to the patio table, *downwind*. "It's okay. You didn't pee on it. Now I can't even take it back to the seller."

Annie tried again, "Even if you have it professionally cleaned? They have special cleaning agents for this sort of thing."

"No, I think the cats took turns at it."

"Or maybe you could resell it and at least recoup some portion of the cost. Maybe they can reupholster it."

Tim joined in, "I looked online, and you paid a good price for it."

Lorna shook her head. There was something else bothering her. "I don't know, that guy Holder ..." She paused. "His attitude bothered me – so blasé – I tell him what happened and he turns it into ... I'm an idiot and when I'm ready to give *him* something come back; otherwise shove off. It was just wrong, like he was reading from a different script." Lorna was working it out aloud now and looked at Annie, "Like I come to you with a question and instead of answering the question you tell me that I'm ignorant."

Annie nodded in agreement, "Oh yeah. You be Holder. I ask: 'Do you like cop shows?'"

Lorna put on her holier-than-thou face and drew out, "*Tomatoes* are in season."

Tim dropped his fork and joined in again halfway through chewing his bite of baked beans, "Deflection! Politicians do that *all* the time!" He looked at Sally, "Tell me Senator what's your plan to help the homeless?"

Sally answered, "Under my leadership, the jobless rate has fallen three percent and that's just in the last quarter."

Lorna perked up. "See? You see what I'm saying, then. His attitude was not just blasé, it was passive-aggressive."

"There's a fine line on the West Coast between being laid back and just not giving a shit. Could that be it?" Tim asked.

Lorna took a deep breath. "No, he was definitely both trying to change the subject and attacking me." She paused.

Annie let out a long, "Mmmm," and waggled her fork at Lorna as she swallowed, "attacking. So whatever he's doing, you've caught him at it. We're just not sure what that is."

Lorna looked over to Tim, "Didn't you say something about the FBI?"

Sally involuntarily sucked in air, choked on a piece of food and coughed it into her napkin. "Sorry. Wrong tube." She had completely forgotten the conversation on the way to the antiques festival.

Tim blinked a moment before it dawned on him, "Oh yeah, when I was a kid we had a neighbor who worked for the FBI, and he'd go around to all the outdoor flea or antique markets undercover, but I think he was looking more for stolen merchandise or things hi-jacked from semi-trucks."

Sally put her fork down resolutely; Lorna was not going to let go of this. "Listen," she started, "it's not like it's a Louis XIV chaise lounge from the Louvre. But you, Lorna, put yourself in the middle of this, and now you're chapped because it's the whole principle of the matter. That chair could have cost five dollars and you'd still be angry. You're not just pissed about the money. You think you can keep them from going down the tubes, but the guy in charge doesn't care and probably made a buck off you. And *that* makes you crazy."

Annie was unsure of where Sally was going with her accusatory tone. Her eyes darted back and forth between the two women. Tim braced himself by lowering one arm to gently squeeze Annie's knee.

But Lorna agreed, "Yes."

So Sally continued, "And if it were me I'd have to admit that I now have a bit of a bruised ego."

Lorna sighed and tilted her head in agreement so Sally went on, "However, I will agree with you on one point, why did Holder say, 'donate it back'? Why would he say that?"

Tim and Annie were fascinated by this exchange. Tim reached to pick up his fork again, but put it back down on his plate, "They must be selling off their donations. Who wants pie?"

"I do." Annie said. "But I'm getting cold."

Lorna stood up, "Yeah, quick, let's haul all this into the kitchen."

Sally began stacking dishes and Tim put the condiments and side salads onto the large pizza pan. Annie grabbed the glasses between her fingers, "I'll start the tea," she said as she hustled ahead of the others for the back door.

Lorna was taking the chair into the garage as she called back to them, "I can get the rest on the way back in."

Within minutes, the two couples were sipping tea and eating the pie in the living room, where the conversation continued.

Annie took another sip of her tea to wash down her first syrupy bite of the blueberry pie and lowered her eyelids, "Whoa, that's sweet. Okay, so we know this guy, Holder, is up to something. He could be selling off donations."

"Which isn't illegal, I don't think." Sally added.

"Or?" Annie asked, looking around at the others.

"Or he could be selling off items that were claimed on the insurance as ruined."

"Which *is* illegal." Sally added.

"Or?" Annie asked again looking at Tim who was delving into the sweet pie, not paying attention.

"Who knows." Sally shook her head, "I mean, really. What do you want out of all this?" She asked Lorna.

"The thing is." Lorna sat up straight and cleared her throat. "This is just one chair, maybe part of a set. Now they had a fire first, right Annie?"

Annie nodded slightly over her tea mug.

"Then the community rallied and donated stuff and the city gave them money. Then they had the flood. But then the city pulled most of its funding. Right?"

Annie agreed, "Yeah."

"So, what if it's not just one chair. What if he's been doing this all along and it's just been escalating. And he's been scamming the old people on the island!" Lorna proclaimed.

"Why don't you go to the police then?" Annie asked.

"She has no proof, really. There's no serial number." Sally explained.

"Well then tomorrow we should look up this Jay Hoozibobit and ask him about it." Annie offered.

"Shit, he's probably in on it too." Lorna said.

"So? If we talk to him and he gives you the heave ho too, that's even more information than we have now, and if he's not in on it he may give you some more evidence. It's worth a try." Annie snickered at Tim who was licking at the purple pie ring around his lips. "If they had to fill out insurance forms for the items then that's the proof."

"You're right, it would have had to have been insurance fraud. At what point does it go from a misdemeanor to felony?" She asked Sally.

"I don't know, like two or three thousand I'd guess." Sally answered. "But – " She started again.

Annie interrupted her, "I think we're going about this

the wrong way, Lorna. It has nothing to do with you. It's not about the museum, it's about a guy who is defrauding an insurance company." Annie smiled triumphantly.

Sally looked over at Tim, who looked startled, which may have been due to the sugar rush. "Just try," Sally pleaded, "not to implicate yourselves in anything."

Lorna finished loading the dishwasher and walked into the living room where a pajama-clad Sally sat on the floor playing with Patience and Fortitude, who were stalking a catnip filled toy mouse she moved around with her hand.

"Hey I need to call Tessa," Lorna announced.

"Yeah, she called the other day."

"When? Here?" Lorna asked.

"No, she called me at work."

"Why?"

Sally shrugged. She tossed up the toy mouse and watched Fortitude fly from the footstool and catch it mid-air, "Did you see that!?"

"Well, what did she say?" Lorna was annoyed.

"Nothing important. She asked if I had my lunch or something. You know how she is."

Lorna did know, all too well. Tessa could be playful, but not without reason. She went into her office and pulled the door to before speed dialing Tessa's home phone. She looked at the time. Oops, she thought, it would be midnight in Atlanta.

Tessa had improved upon the typical caller I.D. Instead of having a phone that rang, her device would read out the names of the callers. So on Tessa's end, her computer-generated voice was saying, "Lor-na, Lor-na," before she picked up.

"This time difference is killing me." Tessa moaned.

"I'm sorry – I should have checked before I rang you."

"Where were you this weekend?" Tessa asked.

"We went to an antiques festival in San Jose with

Annie and Tim.   Why didn't you call my cell or leave a message?"

"Because I was busy." Tessa answered.

"Doing what?" Lorna wanted to know.

"Buildin' a pi-an-ah," Tessa answered.   It was an old southern whittling joke.

"Then why'd you call?" Lorna asked.

"Because on Monday nights I have dinner with Quill and we compare notes on you, and I wanted something to say," Tessa teased.

"Right."   Lorna cut her eyes to Tessa's picture on her desk.

"How's the book coming?" Tessa asked.

"Aside from the title, I'm trying to make room in my schedule to write the rest of it."

"What's it called?" Tessa took the bait.

Lorna delivered her punch line.   "Nobody really likes you."

Tessa laughed out loud.   And Lorna continued off the cuff, "It's going to be a satirical self help book for assholes."   Tessa's guffawing became a wheezing belly laugh.

Tessa was trying to say something but Lorna only heard, "Times bes' sell'," between gulps of air.

Lorna didn't let up.   "My target audience will be people rejected from game shows and those people voted off reality shows.   There's got to be thousands of them now. The first chapter will be inducting the readers into the OFUCA - Orientation for Fictional Unfortunates Cast Aside or something."

Tessa took a deep breath, "Okay then. I will commission you to write it. But only if you keep that title."

The book had been Lorna's pet project for a year, though she had neither the time nor the notion to get started on it.   But since she kept bringing it up, it had become fodder for everyone's teasing.

"Alright, I will then. You just wait and see." Lorna countered Tessa's teasing.

"How's Sally?" Tessa asked.

"She's fine. She said you called her this week."

"Yeah, keep her on her toes. I still don't know about that girl." Tessa offered lightly.

"Right. She doesn't have time to get into trouble."

Tessa laughed a little, "Oh, yeah, she's got to keep up with you. How're my nephews?"

"Good, they're playing in the living room with Sally now."

Tessa and Patience, the cat, had a special bond. Once when Tessa was visiting Patience offered his tail to her outstretched hand and led her to his food dish. Ever since that occasion (which nobody else witnessed), Tessa had showered the boys with elaborate gifts: strollers, cat car seats, hand made catnip toys, and outdoor tents. But the kicker was the feline acupuncture Patience received for his tree pollen allergies.

Lorna rolled her eyes as she listened to Tessa encourage her, yet again, to have Patience trained as a Seeing Eye cat. Although it was true that when Tessa visited, Patience didn't leave her side, Lorna felt the idea was a tad ridiculous. Lorna excluded any talk about what was happening with the Chippendale chair, especially since the cats had peed on it. She just knew somehow that Tessa would turn it around on her and defend the boys. But more than that, she didn't really feel like explaining the whole thing to Tessa. Especially since she didn't have the answers she knew Tessa would be asking to her.

Lorna imagined Tessa's recrimination: "Well that's what you get for bringing a foreign object into their home. What are they supposed to do with a strange smelling object like that? They were just trying to help." Lorna snapped back to the present.

"Okay, talk to you later." Tessa said before hanging up the phone.

Lorna rolled her eyes and hit the speed dial again. Tessa picked up, "Hello?"

"Is this a bad time? Are you *entertaining?*"

"I think I am." Tessa answered.

"I have to ask you a favor." Lorna quickly asked before Tessa did something silly, like hang up on her again.

This time, Tessa sighed.

"Did you just sigh at me?" Lorna asked indignantly.

"But it wasn't a 'tsk' sigh, it was a 'not now' sigh, like an 'I'm in the middle of some stuff' sigh, an 'I can't be just flying out there every time you get a sniffle or hair up your ass' sigh. I'm the *head* of a multi-million - " Tessa teased.

"Yes, you can! You're the Medusa head, that's what you are." Lorna interrupted.

"Oh, you're right, quickly tell me your wish so I may retire to my bottle." Tessa feigned a yawn.

"Okay, you know Tim, right?"

"Of Tim and Annie? Yes." Tessa followed along. Sally popped her head into the office indicating she was going to bed. Lorna nodded and waved to her from her desk.

"Well when you come out next month, he's asked for an audience with you, m'lady." Lorna finished.

Tessa paused, "Why?"

"His company is a human resources firm and they're being bought up by Spectorgies. And he's worried."

"Really?" Tessa was very interested in this. "But last time I spoke with him, I believe he told me he was in an independent firm and they did a lot the human resource work for Colby Systems."

"I guess so." Lorna said. She had not been privy to that conversation.

"Colby is a direct competitor of Spectorgies." Tessa explained. "He's not wrong to be worried."

"Oh." This was new information to Lorna. "I don't understand."

"He might have signed a statement saying he wouldn't work for a direct competitor of Colby, that specifically being Spectorgies, for a certain amount of time and yes, he would be out of work then." Tessa explained further.

"Huh. But here's the thing, he said he wanted to talk to you about an idea he had."

"Oh dear. What kind of idea?" Tessa wondered.

"I don't know, he wouldn't say." Lorna answered.

"Oh honey, I'd like to help out your friend. He sound's like he's in a pickle, but I've got my own ideas in the works. Very hush-hush." Tessa went on, "Patent infringement things. I've got to be careful."

Lorna didn't speak, but scowled a little at the phone.

"Spectorgies is making a move on Colby systems. I'll be damned." Tessa wondered aloud.

"No – he didn't say that." Lorna said.

"They're taking over the company that handles Colby's human resources, what would you call that?"

"Oh. I don't know. A low grade fever?"

"I met the head of Colby once; he's a real dick-head, as you say. Patronizing son of a bitch." Tessa paused and Lorna held her breath a moment before Tessa continued, "Tell you what, would your friend be willing to sign a release form before he and I spoke together about his invention?"

"Well, yeah I'm sure he would. I think what he really wants is the panache that would come with being able to say he took a meeting with Tessa Tollison. Like a negotiating tool."

"Oh no, no, Darlin', these are multi-billion, multi-national companies. If they're going head to head, a meeting with me is like putting a cat on a semi-truck weigh station. It won't even register. What's Tim really like?"

"Good guy, father was a cop, mom was a teacher, he's a human resource middle manager and does some training, loves his wife and dogs…" Lorna rambled.

Tessa interrupted in her all business tone, "That tells me nothing."

Lorna tried again, "He's clever but not obvious about it, likes gadgets, the analogue kind. Plays fantasy football."

Tessa interrupted, "What's fantasy football?"

"I don't know exactly but I think it's where you take players from teams and bet or try to predict how well they'll do against opposing players. It's something like that, like a numbers game within an actual game. He's into photography, but talks more about f-stops than the esthetics."

Tessa interrupted again, "What's f-stops?"

Explaining things in the seeing world to Tessa was second hand for Lorna and did not stop her flow, "F-stops are little points on a camera lens that control the diameter of the hole opening for the picture to squeeze through."

"That makes no sense, but I get your point." Tessa added, in the same rhythm.

Lorna continued, "He's kinda handsome, but I don't think he knows it and I don't think at any point in his life he was a ladies' man. He doesn't get along with his older brother."

"He's got a lot of siblings?" Tessa asked.

"No, just the older brother – and he's short."

"How short?"

"Like 5'8" in heels." Lorna answered.

"That's average. 5'2" is short." Tessa corrected her.

"Whatever."

"Okay then, very good, thank you. I'll email that release statement to you. Make sure you scan it and email it back to me before I leave here next month, okay?

"Will do, and thank you, Tessa."

"What's his full name and telephone number," Tessa asked.

"Tim Doughall, spelled D-o-u-g-h-a-l-l."

"How do you get *Doyle* out of D-o-u-g-h-a-l-l?" Tessa

asked.

"Aah … dunno." Lorna drew out before going on, "555-1115."

"Alright I'll put it in my appointment calendar. Anything else?"

"Nope. All is good."

"Nothing else going on?" Tessa pressed.

"Nope." Lorna's eyes shifted, "You doing alright?"

"Yep, I love you and will talk to you later."

"Love you too," Lorna squeezed in before Tessa hung up. Lorna stared at the phone feeling somewhat anguished. Why hadn't she told Tessa about the chair and the break-in? Did Tessa know about the chair? Sally hadn't told her about any of it. They had spoken before Lorna bought it. No, Tessa had something going on that she said was hush-hush. Lorna mimic silently, "Nothing else going on?" and Tessa was quick to ring off so Lorna couldn't ask about it. "Whatever." Lorna said to herself. She had more important fish to fry with the docent, Mr. Hazinsky.

CHAPTER 7

CHIPPENDALE DANCER

Sally stood at the bus stop, motionless as the fog swirled around her. The dread of what might be waiting for her on the bus set like a rock in the pit of her stomach. She did not see Tim walk up to her.

"Morning."

Sally gave a start.

"Sorry." He reached his hand to her elbow to steady her.

"Hey. Sorry, I'm still half asleep I think." Sally smiled back.

"So you know Annie and Lorna are on *surveillance* today, right?"

"Oh yeah. Lucy and Ethel are going to solve the case of the museum murders today."

Tim laughed. "I thought it was just me."

"No. I get it. I just hope they don't get arrested in the mean time. I'm sorry Lorna's dragged poor Annie into this."

"Annie's not all that innocent herself, sometimes. She plays naïve but she'll surprise you. No, I'm glad she's got a buddy, even if they do get arrested." Tim smiled at the thought.

"Where are you off to this morning?"

Tim took a deep breath. "Colby. They have some training lined up now."

"I thought you only handled their human resources."

"I was supposed to, but they pulled me in last night and then I've got to get to the office in the city."

"Wait a minute," Sally said, "Why are you taking the bus if you're going to Colby? It's like a mile walk."

"Well, when I'm training I like to bring donuts. If you feed them, they will follow. I generally stop down on Warner at The Yum Hole."

"Clever. I was going to start walking to Warner to catch the bus there into Oakland to take the train, get myself some exercise *and* get to work."

"Ah." Tim exaggeratedly nodded his head. "Multitasking. That's why you make the big bucks."

"Ha." Out of the corner of her eye, Sally caught a young man staring at her. He was clean cut, wearing a windbreaker jacket, blue ball cap with no logo, black shoes, blue jeans and had a backpack slung over his shoulder. Recruit. She made a half turn away from the young man and a step back so her focus was more directly on Tim and said, "I should probably join a gym, but I'm too lazy."

"Annie wanted to join The Ohlone Gym, but I'm too cheap." Tim grinned.

"I know, they are kinda costly. Especially when you can just exercise for free, unless you need weights. I wonder if they have a winter rate, like for a few months."

The young man had made his move and did a brush by on Sally, clumsily bumping too hard into her. Tim caught her by the arm and held her upright.

"Dude!" Tim took a step toward the young man, who grinned.

"Sorry, sorry about that – my bad." The young man reached down and picked up a small folded piece of paper, a post card. "Here, you dropped this. I'm sorry."

"No I didn't. That's yours." Sally said sternly without looking at the paper.

The young man shook the paper lightly at her, "No, I'm sorry, you dropped it when I bumped you."

"No. That's yours." Sally repeated, putting her hands in her pockets. There was something unprofessional about this kid, Sally thought, aggressive or desperate. More like an informant than an agent in training.

Tim watched this exchange.

The young man held out the paper at her, his eyes pleading.

"Dude. Back off." Tim stepped forward between Sally and the young man.

Just then the unmistakable metallic hum and exhaust hiss of the transit bus grew closer. The young man backed away, "Oh all right." He nodded and locked eyes with Sally, "All right."

The bus bounced to a stop and people began loading onboard, "What the hell?" Asked Tim.

Sally jerked her head sideways, "I know, right?"

"I'm sorry," Michael interrupted the old man's story, "I'm getting lost. I thought you were going to brief me about this main file," Michael put his hand on a small stack of files, "corporate espionage or something. What does any of this have to do with a chair?"

"I'm starting you at the very beginning, of course. That stupid chair ..." the old man paused, shaking his head, and steadied himself on the galley counter, "I knew the minute I met that girl in the coffee shop," the old man lost himself in thought and shook his head before continuing, "some people are just magnets for certain things and I should have known she'd be trouble."

"Well she gave you the counter-sign, so it's not entirely your fault. What happened with the key?"

"What key?"

Michael felt his frustration boil up.

"Oh, the relay. Yeah, well I figured it was in safe hands until I needed it. When I picked it up I dropped a microphone in their front room and in their kitchen. She almost caught me, walked right past me into the bathroom. I had to kick her cats – it was a mess." The old man laughed at the thought.

"So how did the key lead to the chair?" Asked Michael.

"It doesn't lead to the chair. The key was just the first time I met this Lorna person and I mistook her for my drop. But then the chair was part of a fraud case. I had been working on this corporate espionage case, mind you, some real cold war stuff with insider trading to boot, and I needed cover money, so I opened this fraud case."

Michael stood up and shook his head in frustration, "I'm going to the bathroom. Please, when I get back, try to figure out a way to get to the point." He was very worried. He was a technical guy who monitored the internet, digital forensics, encryption, coding, and now this guy's talking about antiques festivals from a year ago and unstable women. Maybe he's one of those guys who get posted somewhere and forgotten about and goes mad. He looked around the tiny bathroom. Or else he's made a huge mess and needs it cleaned up. Michael thought he and his boss had a good working relationship – why would he put him in for something like this? with this character? He took a deep breath and opened the door.

The old man fought the urge to walk over and punch the kid right in the face. He had to get his attention somehow. He stirred the soup on the burner. The sun had set and the night chill was settling around the boat. "Grab that heater behind you and click it on for me." The old man instructed calmly.

Michael pulled the small heater through the rail that held it in place and set it down on the wooden slats and turned it on. He slid back into the booth.

"Do you know what an oral history story telling is?" The old man asked.

Michael stared solemnly at the old man.

"It's the most effective way of giving you," the old man could not contain himself any longer, "little *arrogant shits* like you, the most information possible in the least amount of time. There are no tidy files to read, no maps, no graphs to study."

Michael opened the first file under his hand; it was filled with recipes cut out from magazines.

The old man continued his rant, "And this isn't about a *chair,* it's about how civilians get caught up in our operations and how the tiniest mistake we make can be catastrophic for them. This is an ongoing battle to keep corporate espionage between corporations and out of the government's files. It used to be they sold guns and stole bomber designs from each other but now they're using information as weaponry with *computers.* Almost every household has a computer now – what if they were all weapons? Now I was *assured* that you were the right man for this job. Are you? This job takes patience, intuition, and most of all, deception. Now, I can teach you everything else you need to know, but I cannot teach you intuition, patience, or deception, not at the level you're going need." He ladled out the soup for Michael and himself and put the bowls on the table in front of Michael.

Michael sat in silence for a moment. This guy seriously needs a vacation, he thought. "This is about the players isn't it? You found a bigger scheme while working on the corporate espionage case, something to do with Spectorgies. What was it?"

"I don't know. That's why you're involved. You're the tech man, digital devices, that's your thing right?"

"Yeah." Michael tasted his soup. Vegetable, and it was good. He took another spoonful.

"Well okay." The old man got up and reached across the galley counter for some crackers. "Then you'll get us on the right track. At this point all I know is that there is some major hush-hush happening in the NSA and the corporations they've hired to update the technical – computers and such. Well, the people inside those corporations, I wouldn't trust them to feed my goldfish."

Michael looked around the boat, "You don't have a computer here?"

"Nope, I told you I'm analogue."

"What's with the second boat?"

"Oh that's yours. It's got all the equipment you'll need on it." The old man took another spoonful of the soup. "It's pretty state of the art in there. When you work on the fraud cases, your cover, you stay in your house or apartment, whatever you got. But when you're working on these cases, you'll stay on the boat. It's safer." The old man said.

"You will teach me about boats." It was a demand more than a statement.

"Sure. These boats, they were my predecessor's idea." The old man chuckled. "He *was* brilliant."

"What happened to him?"

"He drowned."

Michael stopped eating.

"Oh, he'd retired. It was a snorkeling accident in Cancun."

Michael scraped at his empty bowl. "This is good soup by the way."

"Thank you." The old man slurped his soup. "There's more on the stove. Help yourself."

Michael started to shift his way out of the booth and asked, "So what happened with the chair?"

Lorna and Annie sat on the south end of the island in Lorna's car sipping coffee and staring at Jay Hazinsky's blue cottage on Oakside Court. The fog was beginning to lift and dissipate.

Annie broke her surveillance stare and looked at Lorna.

"Okay, what do we say again?"

"We're going to tell him that we bought the chair and we're interested in buying more items, especially Chippendale, that were ruined in the museum."

"Okay, what if he denies it?" Annie asked, her eyes squinting suspiciously at the blue cottage.

"We want to keep the door open to negotiations, so we're not going to accuse him of anything. We want to join in the fun, purchase the items. It gives him a way out as well so he won't feel threatened." Lorna explained.

"Then why don't we just say - we think you've been shafted, and we're going to the police - does he want to come along?"

"Because," Lorna looked at the back of Annie's head where a leaf twiggy thing had lodged in her hair. She surreptitiously reached to pull it out, but then it wiggled, "that would be too threatening." Lorna's eyes grew round and horrified.

"But your way is so 'hey buddy do you want to make a buck?' Sally specifically said do not get implicated in anything and I'm pretty sure that saying -" Annie turned around and looked at Lorna's horrified face. "What's wrong?"

Lorna enunciated slowly, "You have a *worm* in your *hair*." The corners of her mouth turned down as she wiggled her index finger at Annie.

Annie's face contorted as she turned her head slowly around and whimpered, "Please get it out."

The worm was still there, and Lorna rolled down her window before carefully plucking the worm out of Annie's hair and tossing it out the window. After which the two women bounced up and down, squealed, and frantically itched their skulls, until they were left with half teased and mussed up manes. Annie's hair barrette dangled down from a hair nest on the side of her head.

Lorna pulled on her ear lobes, "Oh GOD!! It was a *worm*! How did you get a WORM in your HAIR? Check me – do I have a worm? Was it from the car?"

"No, no," Annie checked Lorna's hair breathlessly, "you're okay. It must have fallen from a tree. It's so awful!"

Lorna turned back around just in time to see Jay Hazinsky emerge from his front door, "Oh no." She suddenly and violently threw her seat back into a reclining position and whispered, "It's him!"

Annie ducked down, her head between her knees. "Hazinsky?" She whispered.

"I don't know, I've never seen him before."

Annie slowly reached back up far enough where her eyes could see above the dashboard, "Did he come out of the house?"

"Yes." Lorna stared at the roof.

"But, he's so *old*. I mean he's barely shuffling along there."

"Who else would be a docent?" Lorna asked.

"But he looks like he belongs *in* the museum," Annie was sitting full upright now. "Old people like that don't commit fraud."

"What kind of fraud do they commit?" Lorna asked lifting her seat to an upright position.

"Social Security, stuffing their dead wives in the basement trunk so they can still get their check." Annie tapped on the steering wheel. "We should follow him – he's getting away."

"In the car? He's going less than a quarter of a mile an hour."

Annie swung her car door open, "Come on, then."

Lorna followed, locking the doors behind them. After three long blocks they arrived on High Street, where on each block, Jay Hazinsky would duck into a shop leaving Lorna and Annie to stare into a shop window or slowly tie their shoes. At one point Hazinsky turned on his heels and headed back toward them leaving Annie to stop and look straight up into the sky and Lorna, in a sudden about face ran right into Annie. She caught Annie falling backward and jerked her into a bagel shop. But Annie was still on *surveillance team Delta*, and said, "I think he's going to the museum."

"I think he needs a prostate exam. He's stopping every block. Let's get a coffee."

Lorna ordered two coffees at the deli, while Annie kept a look out.

"Here." Lorna handed Annie her coffee.

"Thanks. Come on, he's on the move again!"

Outside they stood on the corner as Jay crossed the street about a block from the museum, "Take my coffee," Annie said as she pulled out her cell phone.

"Who are you calling?" Lorna asked.

"I'm going to take a picture of him going into the museum."

"Why?"

"Because it seems like I should."

Lorna stopped, looking at the barrette dangling from the side of Annie's head, and touched Annie's arm with a coffee cup, "Annie, I think we've reached the point of ridiculous now. Let's just go back and get the car. We'll have an early lunch."

Annie balked. "But I'm having fun! Look, I'll go into see what I can find out. They don't know my face. You stay here and if he comes out, you follow him and we'll meet back at the car."

Lorna shook her head, "Sally was right, I set myself up for this."

Annie shot back, "Do you want your 18 hundred bucks back?"

Lorna sighed, "I'd love to just rethink this whole thing. What do I care if old people want to defraud an insurance company?"

Jay Hazinsky emerged out of the museum doors. Lorna and Annie jumped a little as they turned around and began walking.

"Just keep walking and we'll go into the coffee shop-pe

here on the right." Lorna said, beneath her breath.

"Do you think it was just another pee break and he's taking his daily exercise?"

"I don't know. In here," Lorna opened the door to the coffee shop.

Annie continued, "How would he have known it was open. He would have had to call ahead. Which mean he would have known someone else was there." Annie watched Hazinsky pass by the window.

"Refill?" the waitress asked.

"No, just tossing these out." Lorna said as she looked around for a bin.

"Here, let me empty them, we recycle."

"Oh Good!" Annie said with uncontrolled volume.

Lorna touched Annie's arm in a display for the waitress and said slowly to Annie, while nodding, "We need to go now."

"Thank you." Lorna called to the waitress as they left.

As they finally rounded the corner to Oakside Court, Lorna stopped to give Hazinsky enough time to get into his house before proceeding to the car.

"Okay," she said as they sat back down in the car. "Let's try this again. We'll just knock on the door and be honest about this. We'll tell him who we are, what happened with the chair, and ask if he'll explain it to us. ... that we're afraid we've bought stolen merchandise."

"Okay," Annie agreed, "but no last names. You don't know, he could be the mastermind behind this and Holder could be his henchman."

"There are a lot of them in this town." Lorna said.

"Henchman?" Annie asked.

"Old people." Lorna said.

"It's the old military compound. I think they come back here to retire." Annie said. "Let's go."

As they approached the door Lorna added, "I'll do the talking." They waited a moment after knocking.

"I don't hear anything," Annie said.

"He's probably on the toilet." Lorna said.

Annie reached up and rang the doorbell and they heard a muffled yell, "I heard you the first time!" Jay Hazinsky opened the door.

"Mr. Hazinsky? I'm Lorna and this is my friend, Annie."

Annie nodded.

Lorna continued, "I bought a chair at an antiques fair in San Jose this weekend. It's the Chippendale from the museum, the one that sat in the window?"

"I'm no longer associated with that place." Hazinsky cut her off. "You'll have to contact them yourself."

"Mr. Hazinsky, we did." Lorna rushed to get it out, "and I'm worried – how did a chair that was supposedly ruined for an insurance settlement end up for sale at an antiques fair?"

Hazinsky shrugged, "It was probably pulled out of a dumpster for all I know. I doubt it's even the same chair."

"Oh it is," Annie piped up, "it had the same nick out of the arm rest and same material on the seat. I saw it myself in the museum."

Hazinsky paused and looked at Lorna, "Wha'd you pay for it?"

"Why aren't you a docent at the museum anymore?" Lorna wasn't falling for the "deflection" trick again.

Jay Hazinsky began closing the wide wooden door, "Ask Holder."

Annie stared at the front door, "Okay, now we go to the police."

"Right." And they turned in unison and headed back to the car.

As Lorna started the engine, she got an idea, "You know what?"

"What," said Annie.

"I have an idea. You were right – they don't really know

your face in the museum. Let's go back and have tacos across the street."

"It's kind of early for lunch. It's a quarter to eleven."

"I mean, we'll have an early lunch, I just want to see when Holder leaves for *his* lunch."

"Why?" Annie asked.

"Because I need to break into his office and look for the insurance claims."

"What?! No way! Too far Lorna. Nope."

"Just listen. There is nothing against the law. It's a public building."

"Is it?"

"Sure. You distract the front receptionist and I'll do the snooping. It's not like I'm stealing anything. I just want a look. That's the missing piece here."

"Well I'll have tacos with you, but I'm not sure about the breaking and entering. I might need some Twinkies."

"Why?"

"In case we get caught -- I'll need a defense."

CHAPTER 8

ITEM 17

Lorna ate her first taco with zeal in three bites. On the second bite of her second taco she saw a middle aged man with dark hair and medium build in a dark blue suit walk into the museum.

"Shit," she said.

Annie stared ahead, "Where'd he come from?"

"He walked down from High Street. Let's give it a minute. Maybe he's just going to stay a minute."

"Lorna, maybe this isn't a good idea. Anything could happen." Annie pleaded.

"Yeah, but nothing bad will happen. Good things could happen." Lorna said.

"I mean, I don't want to crimp up your plan, but I do have to work at some point and I don't know if I've got a lot of time to be bailing you out of jail."

Lorna lifted her shoulders at Annie, "What jail? Who's going to jail? I want to see their insurance claim forms, that's all."

Holder and the man in the blue suit walked out of the

museum. Lorna slurped the last of her tea. "Ready?"

"I haven't finished my taco." Annie was looking around helplessly.

"Give me three minutes to go in and locate his office, then you come in, okay?"

Lorna got up and left the restaurant and jay-walked across the street to the museum. Annie wanted to use the bathroom and freshen up, but she didn't dare take her eyes off the museum entrance. She checked her watch and for a brief moment she thought about all the work she had left at home that day, but shrugged it off. It didn't really matter; evil Heather would just find a way to blame her for something anyway. She finished her taco and soda and dumped the remains in the trash bin before following Lorna across the street.

As she entered the museum, a pleasant looking woman in a blue chiffon gown that matched her eyes and hair said from behind the reception desk, "Welcome to our museum. Have you been here before?"

"Yes, I have." Annie said. "I was just going to look up front at some the items you have for sale here. Sometimes I find a good book out of print." Annie noticed for the first time that the museum smelled of mothballs and pine cleaner and was horribly lit.

"Well help yourself, then," the lady smiled and glanced back toward the displays where Lorna had obviously gone.

Annie had to distract the receptionist. "You know I found a great read here one time and it turned out to be by Agatha Christie writing under an assumed name." She chattered inanely.

"Yes. I think she did write under several names."

Annie continued, "I just love used book stores! You find so much more interesting books somehow."

"Oh, so do I." The lady mused, "There's a famous one in Berkeley, have you been to it?"

"Oh yeah, I can't remember the name of it – it's on Telegraph," said Annie.

"Yes. Morrie's or something." The woman laughed apologetically, "You'd think I could remember the name of it."

"Well the other one here in town is good too. Just stacks and stacks of books."

"Oh Kevin's place over on Valley. You could get lost in there."

Annie held up a book. "Margaret Truman? Harry S's daughter?"

"Yes, that was one of mine. She wrote a whole murder mystery series set around Washington D.C."

"I did not know that. I thought that was done by one of Roosevelt's kids."

"Well they might have too. But these are bad. I know they were popular when they came out. Let me see it and I'll tell you what it's about."

Annie suddenly had overwhelming guilt for tricking this sweet woman in her pretty mothball-eaten blue chiffon gown.

Lorna heard the clanking of the museum door opening and closing and then heard Annie's high soprano voice. She used her shirt tale to carefully turn the office door handle, which was, thankfully, unlocked. The office was a long and narrow room with a faux wall on her left, like the sectioned museum exhibits. Two cabinets stood facing her, taking up the narrow cement wall, and a large antique desk spread itself out between her and the cabinets. She looked at the disheveled desk and the filing cabinets and carefully pulled the door to, but left it very slightly ajar, in case someone should come back to check on her. Hopefully, she would be able to hear Annie give her a warning. They probably should have worked that out before she broke into the office, she thought. Lorna clicked on a freestanding lamp between the desk and the four-drawer filing cabinet and shuffled through the papers on the desk. Nothing looked important; antiques magazines, bills of sale, a newsletter mock-up, and docent applications. "You're kidding me? You need a reference for this bullshit?" She whispered as she kept looking, but found nothing about insurance.

She opened the first filing cabinet's bottom drawer. It was filled with brass candlesticks that made a clanking sound as she rolled the drawer open, and she quickly shut it again. "Shit." She held her breath for a moment, and then darted to the open door sticking her ear out. She leapt lightly back over to the cabinets and resumed her search. Carefully opening the second drawer, she saw labels that read "docent applications" and the subsequent year, "diagrams" with the year, and "names of exhibits." She closed the drawer carefully. The third and fourth drawers up had sticky pad paper taped to the front that read "Grant Applications." Opening the third drawer up, she saw it was divided by years starting in 1989, with federal, state, county, and city, subdivided into manila folders.

Lorna slid open the top drawer. Suddenly, the whole cabinet began tipping forward onto her. She braced herself with her back leg and hefted the cabinet back into place, while carefully rolling the top drawers shut. She steeled herself for a moment, feeling sweat develop on her forehead. She slid the third drawer shut, but didn't pull her fingers out in time and the sharp metal frame around the drawer stuck her finger. She pulled her finger out and shoved it in her mouth, stifling the cry in her throat, and sucked the blood from the meaty pad of her middle finger.

Lorna looked up at the ceiling and sighed, "Okay." She whispered, "You can do this." Using her left hand she carefully opened the top drawer of the second filing cabinet. She quickly read the manila folders labels, "'Fire damage, fire and capacity certificates, insurance claim' - Bingo." Lorna whispered as she pulled out the file.

"And my third son lives in Boston." The elderly lady was saying.

"Now that's a beautiful town. I could wander the streets downtown all day. So much history."

"Oh yes, my son got us tickets to the Pops when we were there a few years ago."

"Really?" Annie feigned interest, "I'd think that was fantastic – how was it?"

"It was really lovely, but you know how uptight they are over there. So dressed up all the time. But he likes it well enough, he teaches at Berklee."

"How's that?"

"Berklee School of Music."

"Oh, right." Annie struggled to keep up.

"He's a jazzman, that one."

"Well it's nice to have a musician in the family. It's never boring, I'm sure." Annie smiled knowingly.

"You know what's nice? To have a musician with a job!" The woman laughed. Annie wanted to pull her hair out, but laughed along.

"They certainly dance to their own beat." Annie joined in, feeling disgusted with herself. She had spent twenty-five years learning the skill and art of playing the piano and she was being reduced to feeding this ignorant woman in a 1971 Bob Mackie knock off one-liners about musicians' quality of life.

"Well that one does at least."

"Boston, how did he end up there all the way across the country? Is there family out there?"

"Oh no, we're all from Oregon originally, but my husband was in the military so we went all over and just came back to settle here. We liked it the best. Like so many military families." The woman was tiring and became reflective for a moment.

Annie sprung back into action, "Now, see, I think that's exciting. Did you ever get to live overseas?"

"We were in Germany for two years, that almost took our marriage. It's very stressful actually."

"Well, sure, especially if you had kids." Annie agreed.

Lorna thought for a moment. So how did it get into the seller's hands? And was it donated or purchased to begin with? She went back to the filing cabinet and opened the second drawer down. The cabinet began to tilt again, but she was ready for it this time and steadied the giant metal box. She flipped through the manila folders until she found a label that read, "acquisitions." She was running out of time. She pulled it out and kept looking, then pulled out another that read, "write offs." She yanked that one out with gusto, only to have Polaroids scatter down around her to the floor. "Damn," she whispered. She dropped to her knees, flipping over the Polaroids one by one until she found the one she had come for, Item 17. She stuffed the Polaroids back into the folder and grabbed the acquisitions folder. Moving to the desk for better light, she quickly scanned the acquisition files till she came across Item 17. Donated. "Of course it was."

She opened the claims folder and pulled out a manila subfolder labeled, "Fire." She saw no item 17. She pulled out the flood folder and scanned the print out register for Item 17 until she found it. Item 17 valued at $2,200.00.

"Got cha', you smug son of a bitch." Lorna said aloud and then cupped her hand to her mouth and listened for a moment. She stuffed the papers back into the folders and stuffed the folders back into the filing drawers. But she placed all the papers with Item 17 on them into a separate file and set it aside. How did the chair get into the hands of the guy from the antiques fair? She asked herself while wrapping another Kleenex around her still bleeding finger. She began to open the second drawer down again and found the receipts file folder, when she heard a clanking from the front door and froze.

She sprung into action, leaping out of the room in two

long bounds across the office and softly closing the door behind her. Taking long strides, a la Groucho Marx, away from the office door, she buried herself facing a corner exhibit that held an old wooden beach chair and a Tiki lamp. She could hear the clop, clop of men's shoes until it came to a stop. She put her head down and made a beeline for the front door as she passed through the reception and gift shop area that held the garage sale items. She tossed a "Thank you" over her shoulder toward the receptionist and a haggard and frightened looking Annie.

She didn't stop until she had turned the corner and ducked into a coffee shop.

"Coffee?" The waitress asked.

"Yes, a medium, decaf. Thank you." Lorna's eyes didn't leave the street out front.

"To go?" The waitress asked.

"For here." Lorna answered while digging in her pocket for money. "Here." She handed the girl three dollar bills. "Keep it."

"Uh, the coffee's three fifty?" It was either a statement disguised as question or a snarky remark disguised as a silly quip, Lorna didn't care which, and the waitress was obviously unsure. Lorna looked at the waitress a moment and then up at the chalkboard menu.

"Oh, right." She pulled out another bill and handed it over, before looking back to the sidewalk. She looked back at the girl, who poured bottled water into an electric water heater and was pulling out a coffee cup. When Lorna looked back again, the waitress was meticulously arranging a large brown coffee filter into the cup and flipping on a hot water heater. Lorna looked to the sidewalk to see Annie rounding the corner and heading toward her. Lorna waited till Annie was almost to the coffee shop door before she swung it open and snatched Annie inside.

"Coffee?" The waitress chimed up.

"No, thank you."

"Do you have chamomile tea?" Lorna asked.

"Yes." The waitress answered.

"No, green tea, please, mint." Annie asked.

"Sure." The waitress smiled, "That's three dollars."

Lorna dove back into her pocket and pulled out a five-dollar bill, "Here." She laid the bill on the counter as she watched the waitress, who was carefully pouring hot water over the coffee grounds in the filter.

Annie sat at a table facing away from the street and Lorna sat next to her.

"Well?" Annie whispered.

"Jackpot!" Lorna sung beneath her breath.

"What does that mean?"

"They have an entire paper trail that shows the acquisition of Item 17, which *was* donated, thank you very much, to the insurance claim showing Item 17 ruined and a 22 hundred dollar insurance claim filed and check received."

"We know that much! But how did it get into the antique guy's hands?"

Lorna patted her belly and looked at the waitress who was dipping the tea bag in the hot water. "Here you go." The waitress held out her arms to show the finished drinks. Lorna had had enough of *this idiot.*

"For three fifty for a cup of crappy instant coffee, you'd think you'd bring it to the damn table." She locked her unforgiving eyes on the waitress.

"This is fair trade coffee!" The waitress announced as Lorna bore down toward the counter.

"I don't care if it's the rarest ground culled from the poop of mountain goats – treat your customers right and you'll fill that tip jar faster, sister." Lorna grabbed the cups and carried them to the table.

The waitress came out from behind the counter to confront Lorna, "You can leave!"

Annie placed her hand over her mouth, eyes wide, and shook her head at the unfolding scene. Lorna swung around on the woman and stood toe to toe with her. Lorna leaned back and eyed the waitress toe to head, coiling up, "Get. Back. To. Your. Hole."

The waitress briefly averted her gaze and took a step back. Lorna sat down next to Annie.

"I want to go home." Annie whispered. "I can't take much more."

"I don't blame you," Lorna said conspiratorially. "Just, here, take a little sugar in your tea. It'll help. I promise. I'm going to have some, too."

"Do you know who that was?" Annie asked.

"The waitress?"

"With Holder!" Annie hissed.

"No, who?"

Annie was exasperated, "Detective Keeling with the OPD."

"Really?"

"Yes, Birdie told me."

Lorna looked at Annie. "Are you okay, hon? You look a little peaked."

"Do I have something on my face?" Annie asked.

"No, you just said a birdie told you. Just have some sugar."

"Birdie was the receptionist."

"Oh, right. She told you who that was. Okay, let's just take a breather. I have something to show you."

Annie eyed Lorna, who pulled her shirt up revealing a manila folder stuck in her pants. Annie smacked her own forehead and cried, "But you said you wouldn't steal *anything*! You *promised*."

"I didn't steal anything."

"Then what is that and where did you get it?" Annie asked.

"It's a receipt file. Which *does not* contain a receipt for the sale of item 17 nor does it appear on the excel spreadsheet." Lorna smiled and smacked the folder on the table.

Annie looked at the closed file. "Do you think he's German?"

"Who?"

"Holder."

"I don't know. It sounds English. Scottish. Why?" Lorna asked

"That's how they caught all the Germans at the Nuremberg trials. They kept meticulous records. Germans are very good at that."

"Oh my God, Annie, that's so casually racist *and* totally off topic. Have some more of your tea."

Lorna thought for a moment while Annie sipped her tea. The waitress stood behind the counter glaring at them. Lorna nodded to herself before announcing, "I think we've exhausted our resources."

"Me too. I'd like to go home now."

"You don't want to go to the police with me? You'll miss the fireworks."

"Oh, well. No. I guess I can. But what about the file?"

"Obviously, he keeps a computer record of the accounts, so I'm gonna keep this for good measure. The police might need it to *turn up* at some point, and this way Holder can't destroy the evidence." Lorna said, before adding, "What there   is   of   it."

CHAPTER 9

SEAN CONNERY'S WIG

Annie and Lorna walked back to the side street where they had left the car. They drove to the police station at the other end of High Street and parked in the parking lot. The Ohlone Police Station sat across the street from the library, its modern architectural twin.

Annie looked around the lot filled with police cars, "Can you park here?" she asked Lorna.

"I don't see any signs saying I can't."

"Yeah but maybe it's implied – these are all patrol cars."

Lorna opened her car door. "Come on," she tossed back at Annie.

As they climbed the stairs to the front door of the police station, Annie wondered aloud, "You know, I'll bet Hazinsky didn't have anything to do with this."

"Maybe." Lorna kept climbing the stairs to the front door.

At the front desk, they were met by a tall, black, uniformed policewoman who frowned at them. Lorna read the nametag on the policewoman, Sergeant. R. Fitzgerald.

Sgt. R. Fitzgerald took a seat behind the desk as Lorna introduced herself, "Hello, Sgt. Fitzgerald, my name is Lorna Tollison, and this is my friend Annie Doughall."

"Mmm, hmm." Sgt. Fitzgerald slowly blinked at them.

Annie looked over at Lorna who appeared dumbstruck.

This policewoman was *magnificent*, Lorna thought. The last time Lorna was here she had to deal with a pimply faced little shit who couldn't be bothered with her break-in. But now Sgt. Fitzgerald is here and she looks much more competent and so tidy in her uniform, Lorna told herself. I'll bet she found out about the pimply shit's incompetence and kicked his ass.

Sgt. Fitzgerald's mouth opened a bit before she asked, "Are you here to file a complaint?"

Annie started, "We think we bought stolen property."

Lorna found her footing and opened her mouth to speak, but the sergeant waved her hand for silence at Lorna, "Did you buy the property out of the trunk of a car?"

Annie shook her head, "No. At an antiques festival."

Sgt. Fitzgerald furrowed her brow, "How much?"

"Eighteen hundred, but it's valued at twenty two hundred," Annie explained.

Sgt. Fitzgerald titled her head and narrowed her eyes in what Annie thought was deep understanding of their plight. The policewoman bit her lip and turned away from Annie and Lorna for a moment to look through the glass wall behind her. Both women followed the sergeant's gaze into the glass walled room. Wooden doors surrounded three neat rows of desks with four desks per row in the center space and uniformed officers gathered around a coffee maker at the far end of the room. Sgt. Fitzgerald turned back around, smiled at the ladies and nodded, "See those double doors? I'll buzz you in. Ask for Detective Keeling."

"Isn't there someone else we could talk to? Who isn't a detective?" Annie asked.

Sgt. Fitzgerald frowned, "No."

Lorna smiled brightly, "Okay, thanks," and took Annie by the elbow leading her to the double doors and waited to hear the buzzer.

"Lorna," Annie whined under her breath, "he *knows* what I look like."

Lorna remained silent as they moved through the sliding doors.

Annie turned to Lorna, "Are you okay? Having second thoughts?"

"She. Was. *Awesome.*" Lorna had a far away look in her eyes, "Like Foxy Brown and Leana Horne rolled up into one. Like the black wonder woman," Lorna declaimed, "so complicated."

Annie stopped walking. "Casual racist."

"Nooo. I want her action figure," Lorna purred.

"Lorna, snap out of it. Now, come on. He *knows* what I look like. I was in the museum with him, and I was *practically introduced.*"

"So? You didn't do anything wrong."

"But, it's suspicious." Annie's eyes jutted about the room.

"No it's not," Lorna tossed off casually, "you were meeting me at the museum, remember? We were meeting there because I had wanted you to help me confront Holder but then you saw Detective Keeling and decided to just come straight here. Remember?"

Annie got the hint, "Oh, right."

Lorna and Annie stood in the center of the room and scanned the closed office doors that lined the walls till they found the one that read, "Detective A. Keeling".

"Shit." Lorna steadied herself. "Here we go," before marching over to the door and knocking.

Detective Keeling threw open the door and Lorna blurted out, "I have what you're looking for."

"You do?" Dt. Keeling asked, amused.

"Yeah," Lorna answered.

Dt. Keeling craned his neck around Lorna, where Annie was hiding herself, "Don't I know you from somewhere?"

"No, I'm Lorna Tollison and this is my friend, Annie Doughall."

"I saw you at the museum earlier," Annie admitted in a small voice. She indicated Lorna with a nod, "we were meeting there – "

Lorna stepped in again, "We think I purchased some stolen property belonging to the museum."

His mouth fell open and he nodded. He smiled and stood back to usher the women into his office with a wave of his arm. They both took a seat in front of his desk and Lorna began to explain the whole thing to him chronologically, starting with her window-shopping at the museum. The detective did not take notes but listened patiently, nodding occasionally.

Keeling couldn't believe his good luck. He had already typed up a subpoena to confiscate the chair from 53 Saint Charles Place, residence of one Lorna Tollison, and here she was offering it to him. She even had this whole fraud case worked out already. Six months of work and man-hours rolled up into one walk-in off the street.

When Lorna finished, Dt. Keeling rubbed his hands together and asked, "Where is the chair now?"

"In my garage."

"You put a twenty two hundred dollar Chippendale chair in your garage?"

"I know. Patience and Fortitude peed on it."

Dt. Keeling paused, rolling his eyes back, "The statues in front of the New York City Library?"

"My cats," Lorna nodded.

Nothing is this easy, Keeling told himself. I need to run a check on this woman. "And you're *sure* it's the same chair? Not just sorta looks like it."

"We'd both swear to it." Annie answered this time.

"Good," Dt. Keeling stood up excitedly barely able to

maintain his professional demeanor, "'cause you're going to have to."

Lorna stood up suddenly too, "Can I use your phone?"

"Is it local?" Keeling asked.

"Yes, my bank branch."

"Sure, just punch one of the lines there." He indicated the row of buttons on the phone. "I'll be right back."

Lorna pulled a bankcard from her wallet as Keeling left and closed the door behind him.

"I totally forgot about that," Annie said, "I hope it's not too late."

"Here," Lorna pulled out the manila envelope that was still tucked into the back of her pants and shirt. Annie grabbed the envelope and tucked it down the back of her pants, then made a stinky face. "I know," agreed Lorna. "It was totally making my back sweat."

As Lorna accepted the charges for the stopped and canceled check from the bank, Annie looked around the sterile office casually. Framed degrees, a Bachelor of Science, a Bachelor of Arts, a Masters in psychology, one from the police academy, and a police academy graduation picture. No family pictures though, she noticed. Law books, a copy of the book *The Adventures of Huckleberry Finn*, a gym bag, and his uniform hung in a dry cleaning bag on the wall behind the door. Annie scanned the room again. Something was incongruent. She'd ask Lorna about it when Lorna got off the phone, she thought.

Lorna hung up and sighed. She came back around the desk to sit next to Annie again.

"You're doing the right thing Lorna."

Lorna scanned the room and frowned. "Yeah, but I feel like I might need an attorney present." Annie brightened at Lorna's visual inspection.

"What's wrong?"

"I don't know." Lorna squirmed in her seat and looked from his desk to the small bookcase. "It's staged. This room is staged."

"It's an office. Everyone stages their office."

"No, I mean." Lorna stopped abruptly, squinting her eyes. She put a finger up to her mouth and then tapped her ears, indicating someone was listening.

Annie nodded.

"I mean, look, he's got a political science degree, a communications one, and a masters in psychology."

"Maybe he's was learning to communicate and give therapy to politicians," Annie offered.

"Oh, but then he figured it all out and decided just to arrest them." Lorna said as they laughed self-consciously.

They stopped laughing and Annie shrugged in a helpless gesture.

Lorna jumped in. "From now on, I'm buying all my furniture from Swen's Swedish Design."

"They're nice," Annie nodded, "and reputable."

"Right?" Lorna smiled and then said thoughtfully, "I don't like putting old people in jail."

"He shouldn't have been shady," Annie said.

"What if he was paying for cancer treatments, or like, his wife has Alzheimer's?"

"But, Lorna, that's not your responsibility. We all have choices to make," Annie said thoughtfully.

The door clinked open and Keeling walked in leaning on the door handle. Annie and Lorna stood up and turned around. Keeling said, "Mrs. Doughall, Ms. Tollison – may I call you Annie and Lorna?"

The two women nodded and mumbled their assurances.

He held out his right hand and swept it forward, "This is Detective Schwartz, from San Jose." An older man who bore an uncanny resemblance to the purveyor at the antiques festival walked in.

Lorna stepped forward, "Are you his brother, or…"

"I am, him." Grinning, Dt. Schwartz held out his arms out wide for inspection.

Lorna stepped back again. Gone were the beer gut, the slouch, and the 3-day beard. His hair was a glimmering white and cut short in a military style, and reading glasses hung from a chord around his neck. Lorna looked his hair again. It was a very good wig, neat and combed back on the top tapered down around the neck. And there was something familiar about this wig. It could have been the wig Sean Connery wore in *The Hunt for Red October*. Her mind raced to place this memory; she knew this man, she had met him before. Where? He stood tall. Lorna noticed that his shoes had height flattering soles and his teeth were bright white when he smiled down at her. Lorna gave up on her memory search and wrinkled her nose at him, "You sure smell better."

They all laughed and when he held out his hand to her. She took it only to be embraced in a bear hug around the shoulders. "You're a funny one!" He said in a boisterous laugh and reached a hand out to Annie. Annie, being four inches shorter and more petite than Lorna, hesitated to take it. But he only shook it delicately before taking the seat behind Keeling's desk.

"Okay, have a seat." Annie and Lorna sat down as he fished something out of his shirt pocket. "I am Detective Schwartz from the San Jose Police Department, but please call me Dave." He pulled a business card from the pocket and placed it on the desk in front of the women. Lorna noticed that it had an official-looking police logo on it but she did not take her eyes off him. "And I want to thank you personally for coming in today. We have been working in conjunction with several other county and city police departments to deal with these fraud cases."

There was something very familiar about this guy. The thought agitated Lorna. Since hair was the very first thing she noticed about a person, she stared at his wig. What was he hiding?

"So this has been going on for a while?" Annie asked.

"Since the beginning of time, I imagine," Dave answered,

relaxing far back in the chair and crossing his legs. "Usually it's the same people or, I should say, types of people. After a while you can walk down a street and just spot them."

"Oh!" Lorna remembered the parachute pants that Holder wore. "Yeah, I know what you mean. It's like picking out heroin users except there's no such thing as Antique Chic." Lorna looked at the blank faces looking at her and continued, "You know, for a while there was a *look* and people were calling it *Heroin Chic*. Oh! Oh! I just got an idea for the article I'm writing. Quick, I need paper."

Dt. Schwartz frantically started opening drawers in the desk and pulled out a pad and pen and handed it to Lorna who stood up and quickly scribbled several notes on it. Annie was watching Dt. Schwartz, who was watching Lorna scribble her notes. After a moment, she was done. She ripped off the piece of paper and handed back the pad with a Cheshire grin. "Thank you."

"My wife does that," he said calmly to a startled-looking Annie.

Lorna sat back down. "I'm sorry. Um, right. I understand what you're saying, Dave."

"But there's Shabby Chic – is that what you mean?" Annie asked.

"No, Annie, we're talking about fraud here," said Lorna.

"Is Mr. Hazinsky involved?" Annie asked.

"Who?" Dave asked.

Annie explained, "Jay Hazinsky. He was the docent in charge of acquisitions at the museum."

"That name didn't come up," Dave answered.

"Because I don't think he was involved. He seemed to dislike Holder. He might be a witness. A hostile one at that, though," offered Lorna.

Dave took the note pad and wrote down the name. Annie and Lorna glanced knowingly at one another.

"So," Lorna quickly changed the subject, "I just stopped my check to you at my bank. That won't screw anything up for your case will it?"

"No," Dave said, "it's the trafficking – oh," he added, "but we're going to have to come and get the chair. Evidence."

"Okay. I'm sorry that my cats peed on it."

Dave's eyebrows shot up.

Lorna closed her eyes and shook her head, "I'm so sorry."

"You know what you use on that?" Dave asked.

Lorna shook her head.

"You dab up any excess, then put on some white vinegar and let it set. That binds it to the cat urine, and then vacuum that up. Then you put on some hydrogen peroxide and a little baking soda mixed up and let it set. Then vacuum that up," Dave said knowingly.

Lorna and Annie nodded, "Ohhhh."

Dave snorted, "Don't need to buy any fancy chemicals. But it does take several hours. You have to let it dry between steps. That's very important."

Lorna got a sinking feeling and looked around to the door. Where had Dt. Keeling gone? She wondered to herself. She looked back at Schwartz.

"What do you do for a living, Annie?" He asked.

Annie explained and Lorna realized that they were keeping her and Annie here for a reason. What should a cop from San Jose care what Annie does for a living?

"What do you do, Lorna?" He asked.

"I'm a writer," she said proudly. "I write for the internet mainly. Articles, reporting, things of pubic interest." She locked eyes with Dave. Annie recognized the look in Lorna's eyes. Lorna was coiling up for a battle.

Dave smiled at her, "So how did you put this together, the fraud case?"

Lorna said flatly, "It felt hinky." And let the air hang there between them for a beat before adding, "like now."

Annie turned abruptly at Lorna.

"Where's Keeling?" Lorna asked.

Dave smiled apologetically, "This is where we lose 'em," and sighed to himself. "I'm going to be honest with you. He's picking up Holder."

"And?" Asked Lorna.

"And he's gone to your garage," Dave said.

"Without my permission, or even letting me take him there?" Lorna asked.

"Well, yeah." Dave shrugged.

"Dude. First we have a break-in and the police can't be bothered with it, and now you can't be bothered to ask permission. We came here of our own free will to *help* you. And for that you violate my privacy?!" Lorna stood up.

"Wait." Dave stood up. "Please. I don't know anything about a break-in but we have to act fast on these cases. Trust me."

"That's very shady, Dave." Annie jutted her chin out and lowered her eyelids.

"Shady?" Dave looked at Annie and said, "I like that. I'm going to use that," before turning back to Lorna who was headed for the door and saying, "Lorna, give me a chance to explain."

Lorna turned around and pursed her lips at him.

"Just." He gestured for her to take her seat. "Please. I'll explain."

Lorna only took a step back into the room and placed her hands on her hips in defiance.

"Okay, we have to tie Holder to the chair. It's very, very hard to do that, especially in a case like this. Now, we set up the fake antique dealer scenario, staring yours truly, and I bought that chair from Holder. But we can't say for sure if it's the same chair that the museum received an insurance check for, so we can't say that Holder sold it and pocketed the money. It's not like there are serial numbers like in electronics. It's his word against whom? Who would we ask? You see?" Dave sat back down.

Annie's eyes went from Dave to Lorna's and back to Dave's.

Lorna nodded, "You need a positive I.D. And witnesses to testify."

"Yes, but I think your sworn statement and affidavit will suffice. Hopefully." Dave said.

Lorna sat back down. Annie looked again at both of them and sighed aloud.

"I've worked these cases a long time and I've been working this one for six months. I'd really, really hate to have it fall apart now. This guy, Holder, he's good. He's slippery and we think he's pocketed about ten thousand dollars from the museum." Dave looked forlorn.

Lorna's eyebrow shot up. "Ten thousand dollars?"

"Oh, yeah. It's only about seven or eight pieces, but still. Private citizens donated those pieces to the city in good faith. That's why we have these joint city task forces."

Keeling walked in with two manila envelopes and placed one on the desk in front of Lorna and did the same for Annie.

"That was fast." Dave said.

Keeling smiled, bent his arms in front of him and made typing movements with his fingers, "Practice."

Lorna cut her eyes at Keeling, "And you sent your lackeys to break into my garage?"

Keeling stopped smiling and looked at Dave, who shrugged.

"If they mess anything up, my partner is going to be furious with this department."

Annie snickered demonically, "Yeah, and she's a federal attorney."

Keeling's eyes shot to Lorna, "With what agency?"

Lorna smiled, "Does it matter?"

Dave ignored Keeling and appealed to the women, "We just need you to sign these. They're your statements. And your sworn statements about the chair."

But Keeling's voice was measured, "We appreciate you coming forward like this. We are going to do our best to keep your names out of it and also, hopefully, you won't have to testify. I'm going to take all the evidence and files to the D.A.'s office and we'll know more from there. If you'll excuse me, I'm going to radio my team and," Keeling cleared his throat, "get them out of there before you get home."

"Thank you for your honesty," Lorna nodded and shook hands with Dt. Keeling.

Annie signed the statements and handed the pen to Lorna.

"Did you read this?" Lorna asked her, indicating the statements.

"Yes, they're the same," Annie answered closing her file folder.

Lorna signed the statements and wiped her fingerprints from the pen with her hand tucked into her sleeves before standing up and placing the pen back on the desk. Annie stood up and rolled her eyes. Dave stared in astonishment.

"You people still use protected informants, right?" Asked Lorna.

Dave nodded.

Lorna spun Annie around by the shoulders, yanked out the folder from the back of her pants and flopped the soggy folder on the desk. "Ten THOUSAND dollars? Good Luck, Detective Schwartz."

Dave lifted the file folder open and closed it again, nodding, "Thank you, ladies." He smiled knowingly at Lorna, "You, have a good day now."

CHAPTER 10

IT'S NOT ABOUT A CHAIR

Lorna steered the car into the garage and shut the engine off. Both women took a deep breath and sat for a moment before getting out of the car. "I don't trust men in wigs," Lorna said. "They're always hiding something. But there was something *really* familiar about that wig. Didn't you think?"

Annie was really tired and could not understand why Lorna was so hung up on such a small detail. They looked around the garage and didn't see anything out of place. The blue tarp that had covered the chair sat neatly folded up on the workbench. Annie wanted to get home. She needed a nap, or an alcoholic beverage, or both. Annie thought that ending the whole affair would satisfy Lorna, but it just seemed to wind her up more.

" 'With what agency?' Keeling said. Right?" Lorna recounted again. "Like it matters?"

"Does it?" Annie asked as they walked up the driveway and Annie turned up the sidewalk toward home.

"Oh sure. You wouldn't want an ear, nose, and throat

doctor giving you a breast exam, would you?" Lorna said, following Annie down the sidewalk.

"Depends on the doctor." Annie acknowledged.

"Really?"

"Well, no. I don't know. Maybe. No. That would be wrong."

Lorna stopped and looked at Annie.

Annie shrugged. "I am human, y'know. I mean, if it was Brad Pitt –"

"Annie! Brad Pitt does not want to touch your breasts."

Annie smiled and countered after a beat, "I'd touch his."

Lorna laughed. "All right. But you said it yourself, his office was staged." Lorna began to trail off, "...too sanitary..." before she came back with, "obviously they heard the comments I made about Keeling's college degrees."

Annie thought to herself, how long would Lorna continue this post mortem? As they approached the street corner, she decided to put a stake in the heart of the whole matter. "Well, you did the right thing, Lorna. So it's time to let it go now. Let's have lunch again in a couple of days."

Lorna was solidly struck by Annie's casual phrase, *time to let it go*, as she turned back toward her own home. The words echoed around her brain. *Time to let it go.*

Lorna nodded weakly, her body in automatic drive, "Okay, bye, and thanks Annie – thank you for helping." She heard herself say.

Annie waved as she shuffled quickly across the street. "It was fun!"

But Lorna had already turned around and was walking away fast.

The lump Lorna felt in her chest suddenly rose into her throat. She coughed out a gulp of air and heaved in a deep and painful gasp. She held her breath and ran back to her house suppressing the urge to *let it go* and to break down right there in the street. Her hands were shaking as she focused on the task of getting her key into the lock of the front door.

Another heaving gasp escaped her as she threw open the door and swung it shut again, dropping her keys to the floor. Patience and Fortitude sprung to life from the couches and ran to the front door. Patience let out a long whine and began rubbing his head against hers. Lorna pulled herself off the floor, her face a red mask constricted in pain. She made it to the bed with Patience and Fortitude in tow and flopped down – now, the true and deep mourning of the loss of her Mother could begin again.

Sally got on the train at Market and 7th, heading home. She would change to the O Line bus at 1st street. She knew full well she should walk and get some exercise. Lorna was right; she had gained some weight. But it had been a long couple of weeks and her fitness wasn't particularly on her mind right now. She hadn't heard from Lorna all day. That wasn't normal. But maybe no news was good news, she thought as she stepped off the train and stood in line at the escalators to the street level surface. She looked around and behind her at the other weary transit commuters shuffling towards the escalator. A blue ball cap caught her eye. The head looking down was familiar. Sally stepped out of line and let the other passengers behind her go first until the blue ball cap was next to her and she lurched in front of him. Tim looked up at her.

"It's six o'clock: Do you know where your wife is?" Asked Sally.

Tim smiled, "Probably with yours."

They mounted the escalator together.

"How'd your day go?" Sally asked casually.

"I got called out of Colby after I got there and pulled into meetings over here." Tim rolled his eyes. But then put his head down uncharacteristically.

"So the word came down?" Sally was referring to the Spectorgies takeover of his company.

"Yeah." Tim took a step up the escalator and rested his

bag on his knee.

"Man, that was fast."

"Yes, it was. I didn't expect that."

"Do you want to stop for a drink?"

"No, I'm good. I need to get home tonight."

"Me, too. I haven't heard from Lorna all day."

"Really?" Tim said. "I talk to Annie around three o'clock when she got home from the police station. Apparently everything went well. They took the chair and arrested Holder, the museum curator."

"Oh. How about that – Lucy and Ethel did solve the case." Sally wondered why Lorna hadn't called her.

"Yeah, that was my understanding. Did you try your home phone? Maybe she had to turn her cell phone off and forgot to turn it back on."

Sally tilted her head, nodding her agreement, "It wouldn't be the first time it happened." She didn't answer his question about the home phone.

They left the train station together and crossed the street in silence, weaving among the hoards toward the bus station in silence. Sally tried to keep a couple of people between them as she needed a minute to herself to think. Two things just happened and she was struggling to delineate between them. Tim may have just gotten fired. And Lorna had not been answering her phone calls. Was it possible that someone from the Services had already talked to Lorna, blowing Sally's story? Sally could not face that possibility. So, the Lorna questions could wait. Tim said that he had been in "meetings." Were they with the same people in his same company or separate meetings with the people trying to contact her? In a split second decision, Sally caught up with Tim and slipped her arm through his elbow. "You know... if there is anything, right?"

"Right." Tim nodded absently. "What?"

"If there is anything you and Annie need?" Sally finished the offer.

"For what?"

Sally stopped and looked around before starting again, "I'm sorry I misunderstood – I … are we talking about Global Connections being bought out?"

Tim shook his head and widened his eyes, "I don't even know. There were huge layoffs today. Senior guys forced into retirement … it just …" Tim sighed, "It was random."

The O Line bus platform was crowded. Sally looked around and back at her bewildered friend. "Let's take the O-X and we'll walk up from Warner. You look like you need a walk."

Tim followed Sally over to the less crowded platform while an O-X bus came charging through the station and screeched to a stop in front of them, throwing open its doors. "Good call," he said.

They settled into seats near the back doors. Sally got a good look at the other passenger faces that filed past them and finally asked, "So you made the first cuts?"

"Yes, but for how long? I sent in my resume to a headhunter yesterday and contacted him before lunch, 'cause I knew this was going down at some point in the next couple of weeks. Global can't keep the team that worked for Colby Systems if Spectorgies buys them out because Colby and Spectorgies are direct competitors and the team at Global signed a non-compete clause. But then, after lunch, they started calling people into the conference room. One by one." Tim stared off, replaying the scene in his head.

Sally sat quietly for a few moments, then prompted Tim again, "But if you made those cuts today, then maybe you won't need the headhunter."

"Well, around the time…no, it was after I talked to Annie so after three o'clock sometime, the headhunter calls me back and says that I should stay put and they'll have someone contact me in a couple of weeks. I'm watching these guys have their world crash around them. Possibly the worst day of their working life and he tells me to stay put."

"That makes no sense. Who was this guy?" Sally asked.

Tim pulled out a card from his wallet, "Brian Castor."

Sally took the card and looked it over. Brian Castor from Digital People. "Please tell me this isn't a subsidiary of Spectorgies. How'd you get his card?"

Tim looked disappointed in Sally. "I work in human resources."

"Oh right," Sally smiled, but he didn't answer her question. "So why'd you chose him to call? I mean you must have a hundred of these cards."

"He's just a guy I *thought* was pretty effective salesman, seemed to know a lot of people. He always sent me good candidates. But he tells me to stay put? What the hell could he know that I don't?"

"Well okay, but maybe this was just a shot across the bow for you, y'know?"

"Yeah," Tim scoffed, "I heard it loud and clear."

"There's no way to know what's really going on in the higher ranks. Maybe the deal is already done and part of Spectorgies deal with Global was to get rid of certain people."

"What do you mean?" Tim asked.

"Well, so I say: I'll buy your house if you fix the roof and fire these people, the butler, the gardener, whoever from your house staff —"

"Oh right, right." Tim understood the analogy.

After a pause Sally asked, "Did you sign a non-compete clause with Colby?"

"Sure, we all did, everyone on the Colby team. That's why I was sure I was getting the ax."

"Well, then I guess Spectorgies has other things in mind for you. Or they've figured out a work-around."

"Yeah. I just hate sitting around doing nothing, letting someone else decide my fate," Tim shook his head and looked down. "I just want to work. Go home. Live my life."

"Don't we all."

Sally got a good long look at the tall yellow Victorian as she approached it from across the street. The house was dark as the glowing red sky from the setting sun outlined its features. She dug her keys out of her shoulder bag and took a few steps around the front porch craning her head around the driveway to see the car parked behind the house. Standing at the front door, she listened for television sounds and smelled the air for any signs of dinner being cooked inside. She opened the front door to darkness and silence and closed it quietly behind her; she had a gloomy feeling about this. She looked at the green security light. She slipped out of her shoes and coat while looking through the dark rooms for movement and turned on the living room lamp. No cats and no Lorna. The dying light from the day shone through the cracks in the bedroom curtains. Lorna lay still on the bed. Patience and Fortitude were lying on either side of Lorna's still body. Fortitude sat up and stared accusingly at Sally.

She carefully slipped into bed next to Lorna and nudged Fortitude over. He gave her a sharp reprimand mew, but moved all the same. Sally put her arm around Lorna and nuzzled into her neck. Fortitude resettled himself on the other side of the bed. Patience leaned up finally and monitored Sally's movements. Lorna rolled over and let Sally spoon her. "Bad day?" Sally whispered to Lorna.

Lorna moved her head in acknowledgement and said flatly, "I miss my Mom."

Sally held her tight and said, "Yeah."

"I haven't known her longer than I actually knew her. Did you know that?" Lorna said.

Sally stroked her hair. Lorna must have been crying in here all afternoon.

"It didn't have anything to do with that stupid chair. I don't think I ever wanted that chair. I think it was something I imagined my mom would have liked." Lorna sighed. "And I fixated on it."

Sally quietly continued to stroke Lorna's hair. For all of

Lorna's faults and all her unconventional silliness, she was also self-aware and an acute, clever thinker.

"And now I've put some old man in jail for it."

Sally leaned up, "Whoa. What happened?"

"It was Holder, the museum curator. He was playing three card Monte with the insurance company. Making claims and reselling donated valuables, stuff like that. They just couldn't catch him until someone came forward I guess." Lorna leaned up and put her hand to her forehead. Patience jumped down from the bed.

Sally scrambled off the bed. "Hang on. You're probably a little dehydrated. Let me get you some water." She returned a moment later with a bottle of water from the kitchen.

Lorna opened the water and drank.

Sally leaned down to her, "Sweetheart, if you want that chair, I'll go get it for you."

Lorna shook her head. "It was gaudy, didn't you think? I mean, what are we going to do with a random straight back chair with cat piss on it?"

Sally shrugged.

"No, I didn't want it in the first place. Temporary insanity."

Sally smiled, "Temporary?"

Lorna scooted herself to the end of the bed, "Easy, Counselor."

"I want some comfort food. How about ordering in tonight? I'll call Wong's." Sally got up and walked into the kitchen to order from her favorite restaurant.

Lorna took a deep breath as Fortitude stretched his legs out and hunched his back up next to her, "Do you call Wong's comfort food, Forty?"

"I heard that," Sally called from the kitchen.

Sally and Lorna sat on the area rug in the living room, a Chinese food buffet spread around them. Lorna was still in her robe from her shower and Sally had changed into her pajamas.

"So I'm still a little stuck on this Detective Keeling guy. I don't know. It was just unsettling and then Annie said that about letting go and it just washed over me. I barely made it in the door and just collapsed."

Sally picked at an open container of rice with her chopsticks.

"Do you want some pasta?" Lorna offered her container to Sally.

"Chow Fun?" Sally corrected her.

"Whatever. Do you want some?" Lorna shook the container a little.

"Yeah." Sally took the container and continued the conversation, "But it was you and Annie that threatened him. Stupidly, I might add."

Lorna lifted her shoulders, "Yeah, it wasn't supposed to be, though. I said that if they messed up the garage, my partner would be furious and it was Annie who added the federal attorney thing. I might have corrected her but then his reaction was so pronounced. Y'know?"

"How?"

"Like when you unexpectedly see someone you know, like in some random place, right? Your face brightens up for a moment before you realize you've made a mistake and then you quickly hide your reaction. It was like that, but different." Lorna proceeded to act it out for Sally.

"So like he supposedly knows all the federal attorneys in certain departments?"

Lorna gave her *ah ha* face, "But he didn't say department – he said *agency*."

"Semantics." Sally looked at Lorna and raised an eyebrow.

Lorna shook her head, "No. I know. You're right. Let it go."

"Yeah, small towns, honey. I mean I know we're right

next to a city but this is still a small town and small towns get *very* set in their ways, especially police departments. He probably does know a lot of the attorneys who work in town or commute to the city; it's kind of his job. But you left it on a good note, right?"

"I guess."

Sally pulled out a video game controller from the television console, "Wanna race?"

Lorna smiled and snatched the controller from Sally's hand, "Wanna lose?"

CHAPTER 11

YOU'RE ON YOUR OWN

The next morning Lorna shuffled her way into the kitchen, where boxes of half-eaten Chinese food littered the counters. But there was a full coffee pot waiting for her as well. She poured herself a cup and opened a kitchen window to let the smell of the greasy food escape and tossed the containers into the trash, tying up the trash bag. She sat down at the kitchen table and looked around. She knew full well that she should let the chair affair go, but her brain was still hanging on to it for some reason. Why? Everyone told her it was over and yes, logically, she knew it was a done deal. But something was moving around in her brain; the music had stopped, but there were too many chairs and not enough asses. There was an extra piece to the puzzle and it demanded her attention. No, she told herself. She had given too much time to this silliness. She had been sad about her mom and when she refused to give in to the sadness, she created a fixation. Instead of just being sad for a while, she made a mess and put an old man in jail. She accepted the responsibility for those actions. Lorna stood up and put two pieces of toast in the toaster with determination.

She absolutely must get started on her articles today and finish at least two of them. The articles reminded her of the idea she had at the police station. She looked around for the small piece of notebook paper from the police station, but couldn't find it. She looked again through her bag and the clothes she had worn yesterday. Had Annie grabbed it? She wondered. Then she remembered the card from the other Detective. Schwartz was his name. Where did his card go? Lorna checked the time, which was eight a.m. – too early to call Annie. She did her stretches, ate her breakfast, and showered. While she dressed she remembered Schwartz again – where had she seen him before? That wig. She tried to remember seeing him at the festival – had he worn a wig there too? Where else could she have seen him? The bus? Had she seen him riding the O Line? No. Maybe the library? Her brain was muddled with images of him at the antiques festival and she had to let those go too. She told herself it was enough that she recognized him from somewhere and to simply let it go.

At nine a.m. she called Annie.

"Hi, Lorna." Annie sounded somewhat surprised to hear from her.

"I'm sorry to bug you so early. Real quick, did you happen to grab that piece of paper I wrote a note on in the police station?"

Annie was silent.

"Remember?" Lorna continued, "I had an idea when we were talking about heroin chic?"

"Oh yeah." It dawned on Annie. "Right, no, I don't. As a matter of fact I didn't even make it home with Dt. Schwartz's card. I was going to show it to Tim, because his dad retired from there. But I thought you were thinking more about shabby-chic."

"Would Tim's dad know this Detective Schwartz?"

"Maybe, but Tim's dad died a few years ago. Heart attack."

Lorna did not, under any circumstances, want to let Annie know what she was thinking, so she said casually, "Oh that's right, I'm sorry, I knew that. Oh well. Maybe it was shabby-chic. I'll remember it. Thanks again, Annie."

"No problem." Annie said before clicking off.

Lorna put her phone down and looked at the stack of files. "I *will* get to you today," she said to it before picking up the phone again and placing it back down.

She moved her mouse across her desk and her desktop sprung to life. She typed in "San Jose Police department" in the search bar. Scanning through the results, she could not find the name Schwartz. She typed the name Schwartz into the search engine and scanned the results, then typed in both San Jose Police Department and Schwartz where she found a match under an old newspaper file. Detective Schwartz was a thin man with short-cropped hair when he died in a drug bust gone bad. His parents and two sisters survived him. Lorna dialed the phone number listed for the San Jose Police Department.

A computer answered. Lorna typed in the first four letters of Schwartz's name and did not get a response. She pressed zero.

"San Jose Police," a man answered.

"Hello, I need to speak to Detective Schwartz."

"Schwartz? Hang on."

"He was working, I think in the fraud division, with Ohlone Police."

"Hang on."

Lorna grabbed a pen and pad of paper.

The man's voice came back on the line, "Could he be state police, ma'am?"

"Nope. He said he was with San Jose Police and showed me his card."

"Hang on."

The phone rang a few times before a Detective Sanchez picked it up.

"Hi, my name is Lorna Tollison. I was actually looking for Dt. Schwartz, not Sanchez. I live on Ohlone Island and I met a Detective Schwartz yesterday. Is he around today?"

"There is no Detective Schwartz with SJPD, ma'am."

"But I met him yesterday *in* the Ohlone Police Department."

"No ma'am."

"Look I know he works undercover, that's fine, but -"

Sanchez cut her off, "Ma'am, there is no Detective Schwartz working here, undercover or not. Is there something else I can help you with?"

"No. Thanks. Goodbye." Lorna sat still and stared out of her office window at the blue painted Pink Senior Center. Why would a police officer impersonate another police officer? Who would do that? And, then, a bright light bulb went off in Lorna's brain. She felt calm for the first time in weeks. The music stopped and all the asses found their seats. She wondered if Detective Keeling knew as well, perhaps Keeling was in on it too. She wanted to know.

Lorna stepped off the O Line bus and walked the three long blocks to the police station. At the front desk she met with Sgt. Fitzgerald's glare again.

"Hi." Lorna could not help but smile and blush a little.

"Yes." Sgt. Fitzgerald said in her no-nonsense way.

"Is Detective Keeling here? I left some papers here yesterday by mistake and I need to pick them up."

"Let me see... I haven't seen him go out. Hang on, I'll check for you. What's your name?"

"Lorna. I'm Lorna Tollison." She smiled at the Sergeant.

Sergeant Fitzgerald smiled back awkwardly and brushed her hand forward for Lorna to move away from the desk.

Lorna walked over to the waiting chairs and sat down.

After a few moments Sergeant Fitzgerald said, "He'll be out in a minute."

"Thank you," Lorna said from her seat. Lorna smiled to herself. She completely had a schoolgirl crush on Sergeant Fitzgerald. But c'mon, she thought, that woman is absolutely fabulous. Who wouldn't? How did she get stuck with these small town boys? She'll never get her chance with them standing on her head.

"Come on, I'll buzz you back."

Lorna got up from her seat.

"You know where his office is," Sergeant Fitzgerald said as Lorna passed her.

"Yes, thank you," Lorna said without looking back.

Sergeant Fitzgerald watched Lorna go through the door. There was something strange about that woman, Fitzgerald thought.

Lorna walked straight to Dt. Keeling's door and knocked.

"Come in," Keeling said through the closed door.

Lorna entered. Keeling was smiling sitting behind his clean desk.

Lorna smiled back, "I'm sorry to bother you again today. But I lost a piece of paper with a note to myself on it in here yesterday. I was wondering if you found it."

Keeling looked around the floor, "No... I'm sorry. It probably went out in the trash last night. I hope it wasn't important."

"No, that's okay, I think I can remember it." Lorna stood up.

"We got your partner's complaint letters yesterday," Keeling said flatly.

Lorna gave a mental shrug, "Yeah." And? she thought.

"It's not exactly a good way to make friends in a new town, especially after you received stolen goods."

"That I bought in good faith and turned in of my own free will."

"Yes. I'm surprised you didn't call the local paper."

145

Keeling wasn't done with her.

"Why would I do that?" Lorna sat back down – why this animosity?

"Press. Local writer and *sister* of Tessa Tollison cracks the museum fraud case?"

Okay, *now* we're getting down to it. Lorna took a deep breath and mimicked his posture, leaning back in the chair, silently taking him in for a moment and locking eyes with him. She furrowed her brow and squinted her eyes at him.

Keeling leaned forward, stretched his arms out on the desk, flipping his hands over palms up and grinned, "We like to know who are residents are."

Lorna took a deep breath and cocked her head sideways, "That's odd, 'cause you sure as hell don't know *whom* you're working *with*."

Keeling leaned back again and lifted his chin.

Calmly Lorna mimicked his gestures, "I'm not going to do your job for you, Detective – look it up. A simple internet search will clear this up for you."

A flash of anger and frustration washed over the detective's face before he settled back. "Would you mind explaining that to me?"

"Look, I don't want to seem like a crazy person here handing out feckless accusations and threats. Yesterday, when Annie said that about my partner being an attorney for the Fed, that was true, but she works for the FHA. I'm sorry about that. I'm not one to name drop or throw around idle threats. Had I known she was going to say that, I would have corrected her immediately. But your reaction distracted me." She paused for effect. He can snoop into my life but doesn't bother to look into his own department. "It was very pronounced and it escaped me in the moment. You had said, what *agency*? Not department, nor office, nor branch. Why was that? So, I this morning when I discovered the missing note to myself, I realized I didn't have Detective Schwartz's card with me. And neither did Annie. I called San Jose

Police Department. No Schwartz. So I looked him up on the internet. Now there was a Detective Schwartz, but he died in a drug bust several years ago."

Keeling held up a hand for her to stop. He reached into his desk and pulled out a card. He picked up the phone and dialed a number and listened. After a moment, he put the receiver down in the cradle and leaned back again. That flash of anger and frustration washed over Keeling's face again. Lorna watched him intently.

"I appreciate your coming in Lorna. A lot of the departments keep their undercover men, well, undercover. So no, of course you're not going to reach them by phone."

Lorna jumped in, "Yeah, but look. You can't either. Who was he?"

Keeling stood up, signaling an end to their conversation. "I've worked with Detective Schwartz on several cases, Ms. Tollison."

"Which is it? Lorna or Ms. Tollison? Admit it, Dt. Keeling, you just got jimmy jacked around by the Fed, probably the FBI. They handle fraud, I'm certain. They got you to do their dirty work. All those man hours on the city's dime. And I'll bet you *anything* he takes your department off the reports so you'll have nothing to show for it. Or perhaps you just handed those hours over to them. Quid pro quo?" Lorna shook her head, "But what would a little island detective want from the FBI in return? At any rate, I'm sure the city council would see as bad use of city resources."

Dt. Keeling crossed his arms over his chest, cocked his head to the side, and opened his mouth.

This time Lorna held up her hand for him to stop and she stood up, "Save it." She told him. "I don't have time for shenanigans. This isn't my problem anymore. I'll show myself out."

"Thank you," she heard him call out as she closed the door behind her.

"Thank you, my ass," she said as she walked out of the

offices past Sergeant Fitzgerald's desk.

"Bye." Sergeant Fitzgerald said as Lorna opened the outer door.

"Whatever," Lorna said as she left.

"So that's it?" Michael washed the dishes in the small sink in the galley.

"No, that's just the beginning." The old man wiped the cracker crumbs off the table into his hand, and placed the crumbs into a small trashcan. "How these people have stumbled into this mess and have survived, somewhat defies all the laws of reason. She burned me so bad with that guy, I didn't think I'd ever get him back on board."

"This writer? Lorna?"

The old man nodded.

Michael sat back down at the table and rubbed his face. He was tired.

"Listen, I've got some stuff you can look at. It's not here of course. But I've got it for you. The order for this operation," the old man shrugged, "comes out of main branch. Your contact is through Elliot. He's up to date on a lot of this. He's the only other one though. The only reason we've been able to continue this operation going for over 20 years is because we've kept mum. Understand?"

Michael nodded his head.

"My predecessor told me a story once. And I think it encapsulates everything we do here pretty well. In World War Two, one of his missions was to find a way to get chalk dust into Nazi ink wells."

"What?"

"The point of that mission was not to topple the regime but to put another thorn in their side. It made the ink company who was making money through the war look bad, it spread misery among the troops – how can they get their orders out when they can't get their pens to work? – and, most importantly, it frustrated the flow of communications.

That's why we don't make big arrests, Michael. When people get frustrated, they make mistakes and that's what we do here. I frustrate people who are *supposed* to have our best interest at heart. I interrupt the flow."

"Oh my God! Why didn't you just come out and say that?! It's one o'clock in the morning, man!"

The old man laughed and shook his head. "Remember when I was telling you about the hush-hush case from the NSA when I opened the fraud case?"

Michael nodded again.

"Well, as I followed that case, it grew. The CIA are involved, and turns out there is another outfit within Spectorgies involved. I'll get to all that later. But from here on out you are in a special unit of the Fraud Division."

"That doesn't look … I mean, how do I explain it to my boss that one of his techies is going to Fraud?"

"He's the one who cut you loose. You don't owe him any explanation. As a matter of fact, he listed you as a non-essential. At first I thought it was because he wanted to promote his favorites ahead in the ranks but after looking through your file, I realized he was burying you to keep for himself. It happens. Everyone knows Fraud has IT and online divisions, and that's all they need to know."

"So, what now?"

The old man scooted out of the booth, stood up, and walked over to the small portal window. Michael could hear the faint music still playing as the old man opened up the window and aimed the remote at it once more.

"Go home. I'll get the rest of the files on what your new friends here have been up to, we'll go over –" The old man clicked the remote with a flourish.

Michael's head jerked violently down and sideways into the semi-circular booth. The impact of the bomb blast splintered the galley counter top off its cupboard, crashing it sideways into the cabin wall above Michael's head.

In an instant, as the boat shuddered again and slammed

weightlessly in the other direction, Michael reflexively pulled his arms up to grab on to something, anything, to steady himself. He was looking through a tunnel lit by fire and he struggled to take in a breath as his lungs filled with hot gas. With the cabin wall on one side, the booth to his back, and the tabletop on top of him, he pushed his body backward out of the booth. The waterline had risen to his waist. The fire crackled and hissed around him. His heart drummed No! No! No! as he flailed around trying to make it to the cabin hatch. He pushed up with his arms trying to force the hatch open. He seized each side of the stair railing leading up to the hatch with both hands and spun his body upside down using his feet to kick at the hatch, dunking his head under the water line. Choking on the sea water, he flipped himself right side up. The boat was sinking; he turned his body around and lunged forward toward the fire and took a deep gulp of hot air before diving down.

In the blackness surrounding him, he kept pushing forward, feeling his way toward the hole the blast left. It was his only way out. He felt the rushing frigid water on his face and kicked his feet forward feeling his way toward the hole. He kept pushing down toward the rushing water. Out! Out! Out! Something weighed down on his back and he kicked forward, or down, his sense of direction lost. His left arm caught around something sharp, something metal. He let his body spin around and he kicked off the hard metal object. His chest burned and he involuntarily took in a gulp of water. He stopped swimming. Coughing and sucking in more water into his lungs, he let his body float for a beat to find the surface direction and then swam in that direction. He surfaced choking and vomiting seawater; he lifted his head back gasping. Opening his eyes he could see the wood planks of the walkway and then feet stomping by overhead. He wrapped his arms around the slimy barnacle clad pole, clutching onto it for his life. I can't be pulled out of this water, he thought. No one knew he was here and there couldn't be any survivors. He pictured the basin as he had seen it when he walked down to the boats. On the opposite shore was Ohlone Island. He could see the lights on the houseboats. He had to make it there before the Coast Guard arrived. He had to find Elliot.

ABOUT THE AUTHOR

Saylor Billings lives with her family in Northern California.
She is a writer and producer for Billibatt Productions.